The Old Man's Suitcase

By Rollin Harvest

1

The weathered old suitcase was full. Max looked at it with some trepidation. Two lackeys from two different publishing houses had turned up dead from possessing the antique, now it was in his lap. What to do?

Max had lost a lot of sleep, spent an enormous amount of time and perspiration, and now he had what every book publisher in the world wanted---the Old Man's suitcase.

Actually, there were even more people than that that wanted it.

The family.

The grandkids of the Old Man, to be exact. Hell, probably cousins, too. Who wouldn't want a piece of the pie?

The story of the Old Man's lost suitcase was now legendary, a fable almost. Back in the

1920s, before he became an icon, back before he became a name that could be sold to cigar companies and clothing manufacturers, and before he was America's most American writer, he was a talented young author with a best-selling novel on the shelves and coffee tables of everyone's home. The world was waiting with anticipation for his next novel.

The old brown leather suitcase with two snap-down flaps was the home for the next great American novel, still in unpublished manuscript form. The writer had been living abroad for several years and was moving from Zurich to Madrid. He told his wife to take the luggage and he would meet her at the train station; because he needed to say goodbye to a friend before he left. In some versions of the story, he needed to say farewell to a mentor, in others, to a woman he had been having an affair with. The minutiae of his personal relationships on that day have been lost to time, and only the details relevant to his novel remained to be retold through the generations, handed down like a folk tale.

With only five minutes to spare before the train departed, the young writer came running into the Zurich station to find his wife in tears. She had not wanted to carry the heavy thing around with her so she decided to have the suitcase held at the counter. A nice stranger had helped her lift the suitcase onto the luggage counter and he took the claim check from the porter and handed it over to her with a friendly goodbye. As the clock neared the train's departure time she decided to retrieve the case, only to find that the kind stranger had claimed the suitcase twenty minutes before her. She couldn't figure out how, when she had the claim check in her possession.

The young writer, of course, instantly saw through the scam. His bohemian lifestyle had taught him some of the short cons that smooth street operators used to make a living. What had happened was simple enough: the seemingly kind stranger, after hoisting the heavy bag for her, took the claim check from the man at the window, kept it, and using sleight of hand gave his wife a useless ticket he had probably found discarded on the floor. The friendly air and the helping hand also created the illusion for the porter that he was with her, maybe even her husband, so no suspicion would be aroused when he returned for the bag.

The novel was lost.

The writer never tried to recreate it. That would be useless. Too frustrating. He eventually moved on and wrote another successful book.

For eight decades the novel was considered lost, probably destroyed, and became a holy grail for literary circles to fantasize about. Imagine, a manuscript written by America's most loved writer at the peak of his powers. Other "lost" novels of his had been posthumously published, but they were not exactly the pot of gold at the end of the rainbow. They were either novels that he had written when he was younger and chose not to publish because he knew they were inferior, or they were written at the end of his life, when alcohol and depression had sapped his talent.

Max now had in his lap the modern Holy Grail, the Lost Ark, the map to El Dorado, a fragment of The True Cross. He rubbed the grain of the old leather. The corners were disintegrating. Max thought of all the effort that went into getting this piece of raggedy trash.

It was almost three long months ago that Jimmy T. Blick, an old-money Texas oil billionaire, had approached him about tracking down the manuscript. Max was still unclear as to how Jimmy T. had got his phone number, or had even heard of him. It probably had something to do with a mutual barfly conquest. Max was a reasonably good-looking, middle-aged functioning alcoholic that had a voracious appetite for women, and Jimmy T. was a homely old-aged dysfunctional alcoholic that had a lot of money to attract women with. The only possible connection between the two men was their interest in easy bar women.

Most women that came back to Max's apartment couldn't help but notice his extensive library of first editions, as they covered every single wall of his romantically rundown two-bedroom apartment he affectionately called his garret. After his guest's observations, Max would usually lead the conversation around to his favorite American writer, so he could wax poetically about "The Old Man."

That, most certainly, was the only possible way Max could see how Jimmy T. found out about his humble self. The two of them didn't swim in the same pool, but they certainly did go for the same fish.

Max could visualize how the little scenario would've played out: Jimmy T., in bed sipping top-shelf single-barrel malt whiskey with a young brunette, bragging about the expeditions he had funded to find extinct and mythological creatures, along with all the research he paid for to discover the architect of the Oak Island booby traps. He would be sure to boast about his quest for The Old Man's suitcase. The young, naïve, lush/slut would respond: "How funny, I know a guy that's an authority on that writer."

From there it would just be a matter of connecting the dots. Jimmy T. could do a little research and learn that Max's lifestyle wasn't so great. Except for his marginal good looks and his passion for books, he had very little going for him. To say very little was perhaps being too generous. He had nothing going for him. Divorced, childless, motherless, with a degenerate father that went MIA before contracting cancer and ending up dead from deliberately picking a fight with a jealous husband, not to mention Max's poorly paying city job, he had nothing anyone would envy. He was the perfect sucker for a job where the applicant needed to be a gullible fool that was easy to manipulate.

He was well aware of his shortcomings, but when he sat in the air-conditioned Holiday

Inn Tiki Lounge, sucking the scotch residue off the ice in his empty glass, Max said yes to Jimmy T. Blick's ridiculous proposal. Jimmy smiled with grey teeth, his thick blonde and gray eyebrows knotting together.

"Glad to have you on board, son. You won't regret it, and you'll have a great story to tell your booger-nosed grandbabies."

The air was still and thickly rank, as smoking in bars was still allowed at the time. Ice rattled in the old Texan's glass as he paused to guzzle his drink. He gave a careless wave to the bartender that ended in a finger pointing to his glass. As Jimmy T. opened his mouth to speak, his secretary, a heavily madeup, sloppy, but obscenely curvaceous black-haired woman, came into the bar and left him with a file folder, not saying a word. She tried to ignore Jimmy T.'s leer, and about-faced like an overfed soldier, and marched out of the lounge, hips rolling like a restless ocean. The secretary was barely out of earshot before Jimmy started mocking her.

"Hear that?" he chuckled asthmatically and called after her, making palm gestures alongside his mouth as if he were amplifying his voice. "I think I hear pantyhose rubbin' together. Swish, swish, swish. Lay off the rice and beans, Señorita!" He paused, waiting for a courtesy laugh from Max, which was slow to come. "I tell you what, boy. I'd have sent her on this little mission instead, 'cept she ain't got enough sense to know which end of a skunk to kiss."

There is a right end? Max wanted to ask, but could see the old Texan had a good head of steam built up with his observations, so he didn't interrupt.

"She ain't all bad, though," he continued, with one of those exaggerated winks that went out of style ages ago. "I swear, if she could get a porcupine shaved smooth enough, she'd screw it."

Max didn't want to be put in the position where he'd have to give another courtesy laugh to the crass man's jokes, so he pretended to be fussing with the file folder instead of listening. It contained information and leads on the antique suitcase, along with an overstuffed number 10 envelope filled with four thousand dollars "for his expenses," as Jimmy T. put it with vulgar ceremony.

"Jus' let me know when that runs out, boy." He wore a strange secretive leer, a leer a man might have if he suspected you were wearing panties under your slacks. It was the kind of look one would normally ask one's self after receiving it, What kind of trouble am I getting myself into? But Max asked himself only half of that question before becoming distracted by the crinkling sound of fresh bills.

Most of that money would run out that same night when Max picked up an expensive Mexican-Asian prostitute and a couple bottles of Macallan.

......

The next morning Max found himself with a pounding head and a torn up bed. The fitted sheet had been pulled up from the corners and the pillows were on the floor. He had no idea where the top sheet went. After a trip to the bathroom to remedy the pain of an aching bladder, he found the elusive top sheet. It was tied to both the shower curtain rod and the doorknob. His memory kicked in and he suddenly recalled his night with the girl.

Money well spent.

Shambling down the hall, he saw the living room was a chaos of textiles. His clothes and some of the absent woman's were strewn about. She must've left only partially assembled.

Max went through the tedious process of making a cup of instant coffee. As he took a drag on the cup with shaking hands, he muttered, "Damn, I always make the mistake of grabbing the shaky cup." He staggered with experienced grace to his frayed brown leather sofa and set the coffee on top of an improvised coaster, a yellow file folder. Max focuses on it.

Hmmm.

Curiosity getting the best, and the worst, of him that morning, he opened it. The folder was filled with old machine-typed carbon paper copies, handwritten legal pad pages, modern computer-printed pages with post-it notes stuck to them, and a timeline chart.

Clearly someone, or maybe several people, had been working on this folder for some time. Quickly skimming through it, it appeared to Max that the file traced the movements of the suitcase since it had been stolen in Zurich back in the 1920s. Quite an extensive bit of detective work, really.

According to the collected data, the overnight bag had been pawned a few times, lost in a poker game once, traded for services rendered by a plumber, then it sat in a thrift store for a number of years, was also lifted from a john by a madam at a brothel, sold in both an American garage sale and a European estate sale, and then finally wound up in the hands of someone educated enough to know what it truly was. Fortunately for Jimmy T., this man kept the bag a secret and cherished it in his private collection in Bath, England.

The next morning, feeling far from fresh as a spring meadow, Max had himself on a plane to Heathrow with a corporate credit card in Blick Enterprises's name. He had wheedled it out of Jimmy, assuring him he would only use it in emergencies and other kinds of extreme situations. It wasn't necessary, he felt, to tell him the cash he gave him was nearly gone already.

Presently, on the plane, the always unendurable trail of stooped passengers waited in the airplane aisle like some kind of biological traffic jam, clutching sweaty tickets, desperately looking ahead to see if anyone was in their seat (a seasoned flyer's worst fear). It was the biggest irritant for Max's perpetual morning hangover. The heat from the closeness, the smell of too-often-recycled air, the whine of the idling jet, the slamming of plastic overhead compartments, and the elbow jabs of strangers made his head reel and his stomach kick with nausea.

Six rows up and to the left he spotted a beautiful redhead in a brown turtleneck and prayed a silent prayer she would be his travel buddy for the next ten hours. Eventually he came upon her and saw his seat would be much further past hers. Disappointed, he moved on, but not before making a mental note of her seat number. Maybe he'd send her a drink.

Since he was nearly the last on board, all of the luggage bins were full. He knew his case was much too big and would not fit under a seat, so he didn't even try. Instead, he tried to organize an overhead bin so that he could make space for his suitcase. Moving a stack that included a bulky cable-knit sweater and three leather jackets, he knocked a metal cane with a rubber tip out of the bin. He watched with painful anxiety as it fell in slow motion and crashed down on the crown of an elderly woman's head who had been trying to sleep by propping her cheek on her hand.

Her grey head bolted upright with a shriek. Max sputtered profuse apologies, but the old woman answered with a curled sneer sprinkled with little grey hairs. As he stooped to retrieve the cane, still babbling apologies, his eyes met the eyes of the redhead in the brown sweater. She had twisted around to see what the commotion was. The look she gave him was the type usually reserved for flashers at a pre-school.

Frustrated, he raked his hands through his shaggy receding hair. The best tactical maneuver, he decided, would be to retreat, so he said his last sorry to the octogenarian and made haste for the bathroom. He wasn't sure if one was even allowed to use the bathroom before take-off. The toilets may implode at low altitude. They always made such a horrific bomb-like flushing sound at thirty thousand feet; it was conceivable that they operated differently when grounded.

Max stopped in his tracks before he got to the bathroom door. He had found a new love to replace the angry redheaded passenger in 37C. There in the kitchen nook, left unattended, was the drink cart. It looked like a flight attendant had stopped stocking it in mid-stock. Quickly looking around to see if there were any potential witnesses gawking at him, Max spied a low-level threat: a petite male flight attendant who had just turned his back on him. He was yelling in an overly dramatic and stressed-out voice, about people not taking their seats quickly enough.

Max saw that time was of the essence, so he plunged his hand under the cart and grabbed a fistful of tiny Jack Daniels bottles. His other hand acquired several little bottles of Smirnoff vodka, the flavored kind that wimps drink. Oh well, he thought, thieves can't be choosy.

Max scrambled to get the bathroom door open before anyone noticed him, but it was difficult with his hands full of Lilliputian bottles of booze. On his third attempt he managed to flick the little door lever up with his pinky. Once inside, he slammed the accordion door closed.

By the time the "bong bong" chimes sounded to alert everyone to take a seat, Max was comfortable, relaxed from the liquor, and ready to face his travel mates again. As soon as he stepped through the folding door he was confronted by the back of the flamboyant little flight attendant. The man had his fists planted on his hips and was scolding an Asian gentleman who was unsuccessfully cramming a bag into an overhead compartment with all of his might. The frustrated and confused look on the traveler's face showed that he did not speak English, but that did not deter the little employee of the friendly skies from shrieking over and over, "It won't fit! It won't fit!" The berated foreign man probably thought the attendant was yelling, "You can do it! You can do it!" because he just kept pushing harder. Finally, the little attendant, who couldn't resist the opportunity to condescend, said, "Hel-loooo? What do you not get? It won't fit!" He then looked around smugly at his audience, thinking he was going to get a round of applause for his cutting-edge comedy stylings.

To Max's delight, the Asian man finally won the bout with the flight attendant by getting the bag to fit. Max tapped the rude little man on the shoulder so he could squeeze by him. As he nudged past he said, "Why don't you pick on someone who speaks your own language?" Ignoring the man's look of mock shock, and glancing at the mustard-colored cravat he wore to accessorize his outfit and stand out from his co-workers, Max said, "Nice neckerchief, by the way."

Max knew his food and drink service was going to be nonexistent now, but he felt compelled to defend those that were on the same path as he.

Fishing around in his pocket, for he couldn't remember his seat assignment, Max found his ticket. As fortune would have it, his seat, 45E, was wedged between a fat woman sleeping with her face smeared against the window and, his favorite, the mustached old lady.

"Oh." Max said to the woman. "That was your cane."

"Yes," she said shortly, with her eyes nearly crossed from irritation.

As he climbed over her he muttered, "It seems I must suffer the slings and arrows of outrageous fortune." She grunted out an irked sound as she shifted her knees to accommodate his passing and then tilted her seat back and closed her eyes.

Two hours later, after listening to the stereophonic treat provided by the two women performing a duet of snores on either side of him, Max gave up trying to read *Ten Years After* by Dumas. Frustrated, because he was looking forward to re-reading all of the novels about Athos, Porthos, and Aramis in chronological order, he now had nothing to take his mind off his discomfort. He really needed to pay the bathroom a visit but did not want to anger the lady any further by climbing over her. Instead, he tried daydreaming.

The first thought that came to him was a memory, a memory from childhood, of another flight. He was nine years old and his mother, most likely tired of him, sent him to spend the entire summer with an aunt in Ohio. Aunt Betty, still called "Aunt Birdy" by Max, a moniker that stuck since he couldn't say her name correctly when he was three, was okay as far as aunts went, but she was only a little more attentive than his inattentive mother. She called him "Nax" in retaliation for her Birdy nickname. Originally, Nax was an affectionate sobriquet, but over time it evolved into a passive way for her to needle the boy.

Max was generally left to his own devices, since Betty was frequently busy getting to know her new boyfriend in her bedroom. So he spent most of the summer reading comic books, usually ones featuring vampires or werewolves, along with Tom Swift and Three Investigator novels. The remainder of the time was spent wandering around Aunt Birdy's huge backyard and the wooded area bordering it, where his lonely imagination would create all kinds of horror and enchantment. He took well to the outdoors and began to read his books and comics outside under a tree—not only because he enjoyed it but because it got him away from the rhythmic clatter of the wall his room shared with Aunt Birdy's.

When summer was over and it was time to return, Max became anxious about returning home. He hadn't been homesick at all for the past two months. He hadn't been content either. Just sort of numb. What was causing the anxiety was the prospect of the flight alone.

In those days, children who flew alone were escorted to their seat by an airline employee, and if they needed to transfer in another city, another employee would be there to lead the child to the connecting flight. With divorce becoming increasingly popular in America, it became frequent that the overtaxed employees let things fall through the cracks and kids had to make their own connections solo. This nearly happened on his flight to Ohio, but the stewardess, late to the plane, found him roaming around near the exit.

However, on Max's return trip he got off at O'Hare and saw there was no one waiting for him again, but he knew that this time he didn't have time to wait. Sitting on the tarmac too long had reduced his connection time to five minutes. He ran, looking for an arrivals and departures sign. Eventually finding one, he orientated himself, saw that the gate numbers were descending, and ran in that direction.

When he arrived out of breath at the gate, the young woman told him he was too late and the jet's door would not be reopened once closed. Max felt panic claw its way up his throat from his stomach and his eyes began to fill with water. He would not let this pretty lady see him cry. He fought his emotions and didn't allow himself to blink, in the hope that the tears brimming in his lower lids would dry up and not run down his cheeks.

The airline woman found another flight for him, but unfortunately, she said, it was not for another six hours. He thanked the lady and went straight to the new gate, as he had an unreasonable fear that he would miss the flight if he stopped for even a second. He thought with all certainty that if he dawdled he would use up the entire six hours looking for the gate and then be in the same boat again.

Near the gate, frantic, Max found a bank of pay phones and slid himself onto the plastic seat of one, fishing change out of his corduroy pockets. Sweaty fingers fumbled and dropped two coins down the crack between the seat and the adjoining wall. *No! Now I won't have enough to call.* He still had five quarters and a dime. Hopefully that would be enough. He had no idea how much a phone call would cost. Max saw it before his eyes—his mother getting to the airport, angry that he wasn't on the plane, and then having to drive all the way home. She'd be furious. Or worse, he'd be stuck in O'Hare forever. After depositing the change, the phone clicked a couple times and then began to ring.

She didn't answer and his panic grew, thinking that she may have already left to pick him up at the airport. She would have no way of knowing he had missed his flight. He tried to calm himself, tell himself that she wouldn't leave that early to get him since he wasn't due to land for another three hours. But maybe she had gone shopping and was planning on heading to the airport straight from the mall. She'd never get his call.

He'd wait twenty minutes and then try to reach his mother again. His nerves didn't allow him to wait that long and he called again after only five.

To his relief, she picked up on the fifth ring. She didn't sound concerned at all. In fact she sounded irritated and acted like it was Max's fault he missed his connection.

There were no words of comfort or sympathy or, what he really needed, advice about what to do, and reassurance that he would catch the next flight and everything would be just fine. Instead she sighed heavily and said she'd be there and hung up on him.

Max was brought back from his memory by an airline attendant—thankfully, not the sarcastic little man—who wanted to know if he needed any coffee. Although it would test his bladder, he asked for a whiskey.

As the attendant walked away, waddling a bit because she carried a little too much weight in the thighs, Max reflected on how much the world had changed since he was nine years old. When he was a child, the attendants were called stewardesses and they were required to be attractive. Equal opportunity employment sure took the fun out of travel.

After an uncomfortable ten-hour flight, which whiskey and fruity malt beverages couldn't alleviate, Max found his luggage and left the airport in a Fiat he had rented, or "hired" as the English would say, and tried to stay on the correct side of the road. Also, it seemed he would need to learn a second language. "Give way" meant yield, and "way out" meant exit. What an overly verbose people, he thought. They have two words to America's one. We must be far more efficient as a country, or, at the least, more succinct and to the point.

He was fascinated by London and wished he could stop and enjoy it. All of the history, the art, the famous writers and their homes that had been turned into museums had always fueled his imagination. He had heard of a bar in the neighborhood where the likes of Dickens and Shakespeare had lived, a bar they had most certainly gone to, and Max had always wanted to visit it. To think that a bar had stayed a bar for hundreds of years amazed him, especially since he was from a land where one month a building was a grocery store, then a bookstore, and then a Walmart. In America nothing stayed the same, and the little bit of history the country did have had rarely been respected—unless a buck could be made off it, of course.

As a teenager overlapping into manhood, he had a strong fascination for the Wild West. Doing his own research, he found that Wyatt Earp had at some point after the famous gunfight at The O.K. Corral come to San Diego and bought some buildings for gambling and prostitution businesses. Max was appalled to discover that it was very difficult to find the addresses of these historic buildings, and when he finally did, they were not marked at all for the purpose of maintaining history. It was many years later that he drove by one of the buildings and saw that someone had bought it and put up an enormous shiny brass sign: "Wyatt Earp's Old-Time Saloon and Restaurant." Advertizing a slice of history to sell a slice of bread. Max was happy the building was at least finally appreciated as a landmark of sorts.

The English sky began to drizzle dirty grey drops on Max's little Fiat. As the wipers pushed the water around his windshield like oil, he tried to concentrate on staying on the left side of the road. It was an especially hard chore whenever he had to make turns onto connecting streets.

The ashy grey city briefly gave way to suburbs of row houses, then to an industrial area, and then finally endless fields of murky green with a grey slash of sky along the

horizon line. Eventually, after getting lost
several times, he found his way, and soon the
sun struggled out of the clouds to make its
presence known, though it didn't really assert
itself very well.

He rolled down asphalt paths on thickly
grassed slopes, then up into his destination
town, Bath. He didn't find the yellow-colored
town as charming as the swarms of tourists
did. In fact, he was miserably cranky. At a
kiosk he gained a listing of hotels and bed
and breakfasts. (Also, he learned from a
nearby tour guide with a booming voice and a
red-veined nose that the town was yellow due
to the unique ore that was mined from the
earth and used for building.) After visiting
several hotels that were full, Max found
himself a "charming" antique hovel of a hotel
room. Tired and irritated, all he wanted was
to pee and go to sleep. Two very simple

pleasures. The first pleasure was not possible to accommodate, so Max called down to the front desk, and in plain offensive American English demanded to know where the toilet was in his room.

It was going to be a bad trip.

The next morning, after shaving, bathing, and peeing in a communal bathroom one floor above his room, he went to make inquiries about Thomas Willburry Sleeveridge, the current owner of the Old Man's suitcase. He briefly wondered why Jimmy T. hadn't just sent one of his own employees, someone other than his bovine-brained secretary, to fetch the case, since it seemed to be such a simple task. But the fleeting thought passed when a woman in lacquered-on pants walked by and set his mind down a different avenue.

At the same little visitor's information kiosk he stopped at the day before, he found what he needed: a map, an address for the mansion, and the morning newspaper, which happened to be running an article on Sleeveridge. Apparently he had died a week ago.

Surely Jimmy T. must've been aware of this fact. How could he let a ragingly important detail like that go unsaid? Should he call the overly aggressive Texan and put him on the spot? A conversation with him wasn't an experience one really relished. Maybe he should just ride it out a little while and see what happened. Obviously he was sent to England to see a dead man for a reason.

One moment he was willing to play Jimmy T.'s game, and the next he'd thought better of it. He kept vacillating between the two. Why did things always have to be so complicated? Nothing was going right, so Max found a pub to get his "morning sea legs," as he called it, and as always, accused the bartender of giving him "the shaky cup."

Not having any clear ideas on how to proceed after experiencing an obstacle such as death, after his morning bracer, Max drove out to the old manse anyway, even though there wasn't a living soul there. The ride was brief, along a meandering road that curved through a green hillside flecked with quickly drying dew and the occasional fluffy patch of sheep. At first glance they looked like albino tumbleweeds, roaming around in a choreographed group. On a small bluff, a steep horseshoe-shaped gravel drive led up to the grand yellow façade that was somewhere in size between a shanty and a castle.

Several men were milling about in the gravel, loading furniture into a covered truck. After snooping around, pretending to be an antiques buff, Max approached a stiff-faced, wiry-haired balding man in tails and concluded he was the butler.

"So, hello there. Are you going to have a garage sale or take this stuff to a swap meet?" Max asked confidentially, like he was trying to get the inside scoop on the winner of the ninth at Aqueduct.

The bewildered man blinked a good ten times and then said he didn't understand the language he used, so Max switched to the language that has no accent and slipped Thomas Willburry Sleeveridge's butler a traveler's check, telling him to notify him at his hotel when they decided to have an estate sale. He told the elderly manservant that he was on the lookout for a Chippendale's hutch.

The logical thing at this point was to call Jimmy T. and ask why he was sent to meet Willburry Sleeveridge when the man was dead, but Max decided he didn't want to go back home just yet, so he scratched the idea once again of phoning America. Back in town, with no clue as what to do, but wanting a free vacation, Max passed the time by chasing skirts, pants, shorts, skorts, kulats—he wasn't picky—and drinking premium whiskey on Jimmy T.'s dime. The whiskey flowed aplenty, but the sex barely trickled. In the two weeks he stayed in the little town waiting for the estate sale, he only bedded one middle-aged backpacking tourist. Not his personal best.

Max met her in a pub that sported incredibly huge wood beams supporting a very low ceiling, lots of brass railings, and the largest selection of whiskey he had ever seen. He noticed her almost right away, sitting alone at the end of the bar and bending the bartender's small lobeless ear while nursing a very dark beer. An enormous backpack with an attached sleeping bag leaned against her stool. She was wearing a tight lime-green tank top, which was fortunate for Max, since he could make sure she shaved under her arms.

Years later when he'd tell the story, he'd refer to her as Gladys, but in truth he could not remember her given name. Gladys was a straight-haired brunette just outside the neighborhood of forty-five, but that neighborhood was on the right side of the tracks, as she was blessed with a fit, slim build. She had pretty eyes, dull, lifeless hair, a sort of plain face with an overbite that he found oddly appealing, and a long nose a bit on the large side. Max was okay with her nose, because he had a theory, one he loved to propagate in bars with his drinking buddies. The men would laugh and agree and nod their heads while their wives and girlfriends would always scowl at him and call him an ass. Once he was even slapped.

His theory ran that if a woman is genetically gifted with an attractive figure, face, and such, but she's born with a big nose, then, because she is so close to being a knockout but falls just short a few frustrating inches away from the finish line, that woman tries harder and overcompensates in many areas. If you look around the gym, Max would say to illustrate his point, the extremely attractive girls are taking it easy on the equipment, but the nearly hot girls are working twice as hard because they are frustrated that they are almost to the other girls' level, but falling a little bit short. It's the same thing in bed, he'd muse: a beautiful woman will often not try very hard, because she feels that her lover should count himself lucky. She feels she is gracing him with her presence. The woman with the big nose, however, will be pulling out tricks that are practiced only in the remotest parts of Thailand.

Gladys sort of proved Max's theory. She wasn't amazing, but she was not bad at all. He had filled her up with half a bottle of whiskey before suggesting they check out the view from his alley-side room. They were both so starved for ephemeral companionship that they didn't bother turning down the bed spread and fell onto it in a tangled panting heap. Gladys, surprisingly, stayed the entire night. He imagined she loved the change from sleeping on the cold hard ground.

Max started reporting to Jimmy T. every two or three days, explaining that there hadn't been an estate sale yet. The Texan's first explanation of why he hadn't informed Max of the Sleeveridge death was so roundabout

and confusing Max felt as if he had just
watched a political debate. But the phone
conversations were always tiresome. Jimmy T.
wanted Max to be "proactive"—break into the
mansion and abscond with the luggage in the
night like an eloping teenage girl. Max was a
low-life, and he knew it, but he couldn't
bring himself to break into a home with the
intent to burgle. He might sleep with a
married woman, or date a near minor, or even
pick up a woman at her husband's funeral, but
he drew the line at playing Boston Blackie.
After all, a man has to have *some* principles.

2

On his fourteenth day in Bath, the day after he conquered the mountain climber, Max opened the paper to read: "Willburry Sleeveridge Manor Burgled."

Crap.

The article read that nothing seemed to be missing, but all the closets were thoroughly tossed.

Now the Texas oil billionaire would be very upset. The suitcase was surely stolen; it was the type of item that old family members and housekeepers and faithful retainers wouldn't notice went missing.

Max was at a total loss. He turned the problem over and over in his mind and couldn't come up with any solution. One thing he did know was that he did not want to call the

Texan. How could he find the suitcase? He wasn't a professional detective. Max didn't know what the first step would be in tracking someone or something. Why the hell did Jimmy T. hire him? Sure, he knew how to enter an estate sale, pay for an item, and then fly back home with it. *That* he could handle. He had bought many items in his life, with relative ease even, but to have something stolen from almost right beneath his nose, and then to have to track it through a foreign country, was beyond his experience.

Max needed a drink.

He walked across the street to a small café named after some forest creature's head and ordered an Irish coffee. He stared blankly into the cup, hoping for some tealeaves to float to the surface so he could read the answer to his problems. His mind began to wander and jump from one problem to the next.

The stupid suitcase assignment was really just the tip of the iceberg for Max.

People will say they are stuck in a dead-end job, but Max was stuck in a dead-end life. Like most people, he could trace his problems back to his childhood. Not the happiest time, to be sure. His parents were very neglectful. At an early age he learned to immerse himself in a fantasy world of reading. No matter how bad things got, he always had his books.

Oddly enough, Max had learned to read from television. He was five years old, had very little interest in school, and was far behind everyone in his class. One day he discovered a Japanese channel on their old TV set. He could remember sitting there, alone on the edge of his parent's bed, with his jaw dangling open, as he saw costumed heroes in colorful tights jumping around, administering powerful flying kicks and shooting laser beams

out of their opened palms. There were words at
the bottom of the screen that he knew
explained what these guys were saying, but he
couldn't read them. He'd catch the occasional
word, like "man" or "stop," but he couldn't
read the little white letters fast enough as
they whizzed by. His mother explained that it
was a Japanese program, but she never seemed
to have time to read the words to him. He
asked a Japanese woman who lived down the
street from him what the words were about. She
explained that they were called subtitles. Max
inquired if she could read them to him. She
didn't read English very well, she said, but
she could tell him what was being said since
she spoke Japanese. So they made a date for
the next time the show aired.

The next week came and Max and his
middle-aged neighbor sat on the edge of Mom

and Dad's bed while she interpreted what was being said. Max was so excited.

He went to school and focused on learning to read. It was soon after he mastered the subtitles that he discovered comic books on a metal spinning rack down at the Rexall Drug. The four-color adventure stories fueled Max's reading addiction. From there it was Three Investigator's novels and Encyclopedia Brown. Eventually he advanced to hardboiled mysteries like Mike Hammer and Michael Shayne, and even his mother's Ellery Queen books.

He read the Old Man's books in high school, but couldn't appreciate them. Max didn't like to be forced to do things, and required reading in school was something to be resisted. *Jane Eyre*, *Siddhartha*, *Return of the Native*…all of it was a roadblock that kept him from reading the things he truly wanted to. And the biggest obstacle of all was the Old

Man. He came to look at America's greatest writer as an enemy, torturing him with boredom. It was years later, as an adult, that he developed his passion for the man's writing.

Max recalled a sleepless night in his early twenties, when he turned on the late show and saw a terrific black-and-white film noir. He was so impressed with the movie that he researched the writing credits at the library the next day and discovered it was based on a short story by his old high school nemesis. Curiosity piqued, he made a beeline for the card catalog and found the short story. The rest was blissful history.

The Old Man's writing sparked something inside of Max that made him want to put pen to paper and attempt to write fiction himself. He would start short stories but seldom finish them.

Currently he was working an extremely uneventful job with the city. Day after day he created spreadsheets and entered dreary data. His soul was crying out from the lack of creativity in his life. Max sat directly across from his boss, but since she couldn't see the front of his computer screen, he began working on a novel. At first he would come in and start the day by zipping through his data-entry work so he would have the rest of the day after lunch to work on his novel; if his supervisor ever came around to his side of the desk, he would quickly minimize the screen to hide his writing. Eventually he became so involved in his novel, and so disenchanted with his job, that he stopped doing his work altogether, and would just write for the entire eight-hour day.

Max knew that it was a matter of time before someone realized that he hadn't generated any real work and he would be fired. He just couldn't help himself. He had been sucked into the imaginary world that he created. It was a vortex that he wasn't strong enough to swim against.

The novel was about a failed potato farmer in the 1920s who was forced to take an entry-level position in a condom factory. The character ends up having a steamy affair with a Norwegian immigrant who also works there. It was light, fluffy fare and Max was aware of it. He was quite shallow. The Old Man could spill emotion onto the page, using combinations of words that felt freshly strung together. There was such power in his words. Even if they were feelings that Max had never felt before, he felt them when he read the man's books. Now *there* was a complex individual! The sad thing was that Max knew he could never be as talented as his hero. He just wasn't emotionally complex enough. Why even try?

Max snapped out of his reminiscence. The tealeaves floated up in his cup.

I'll go chat up that Jeeves fellow at the Willburry Sleeveridge home, he thought to himself.

......

Max pulled into the thickly graveled drive with his rented Fiat and deliberately parked it next to a dark blue late-model Bentley. That living cliché of a butler must've heard Max pull up, for he answered the door immediately, irritated under his calm English manservant facade. Max wasn't going to let the man's attitude ruin the good head of steam and sudden burning ambition he had worked up. He opened with small talk.

"Hi. How ya been, my good man…Godfrey?"

"How may I help you, sir?" he answered, ignoring the flippant nickname Max had given him.

"I saw about that robbery in the paper. Tough luck, there. Say, since they didn't really get anything are you still going to have that…"

"Garage sale, sir? I have since learned the definition of the word from your American *Matlock*."

"Ah, a fine fellow, that Matlock," Max declared. "I went to school with his sister on his mother's side. A wonderful girl, Lippy was. She started the Lippy Lock Orphanage for Children with Verbally Challenged Parents. A great cause, but you've gotten me off topic, sir. I figure a Chippendale's hutch would be difficult for a thief to get out a window, so maybe you'd be having that sale still?"

The stately old gentleman said there had indeed been enough interest so the family had been considering an estate sale by appointment only.

Max hung on the words "enough interest." He asked if any other antique lovers had been inquiring about dibs on estate sale items, and, sure enough, old Pennyworth recollected a tall skinny man with an excellent tan and a thin comb-over hairdo who came by twice. It seemed that the man was interest in Japanese porcelain and old steamer trunks.

Old steamer trunks? The brilliant bastard. Why hadn't Max thought of that? What had he asked about for himself? A Chippendale's hutch? His skinny rival was obviously much better at this game than he, for the man had requested not the specific item he wanted, which would have created suspicion, but something similar to it so it would be the butler's idea when he suggested the suitcase. And it worked, for old Jarvis helped out the skinny vain man by telling him that, though he had no Japanese porcelain, there were some fine specimens of Mallorca ceramic ware and an old turn-of-the-century suitcase.

Max saw how it all fit. Once the culprit found out the suitcase was in the house, he came back at night and took it. Since he didn't pay for it, there was no inspection of its contents and no record of his purchase, so ownership of it couldn't be traced to him.

Max asked the butler if he had any contact info on the gent because he had a boatload of Japanese porcelain he wanted to unload.

Bingo.

The butler excused himself and then returned with a hotel business card with no name but the number 142 jotted on the back. Apparently, tall, dark, and balding had, on his first visit, come up with the same spiel Max had used about contacting him if items were going up for auction, and left the card, which was a bad move.

"I'm turning into a regular Sam Spade," Max said to himself with pride.

He found the hotel with no problem. Ironically, it was only a block away from his humble room. Max noted that it was a larger and nicer building than his. At the reception desk the little French man said that room 142 had checked out that morning. Most certainly he'd be told no if he asked for the name of the occupant, but he had to make an attempt anyway. Sure enough he was politely told the hotel was not allowed to divulge any personal information about their guests.

Max needed a trowel to peel his face off the brick wall he had smacked into. Now what, Mr. Hotshot, PI?

Max walked out onto the crowded doublewide sidewalk and wandered aimlessly among the tourists. A bar was in order. He ambled into the first one he came to and asked if they stocked any single malt from Islay. The bartender produced a glass of Bowmore, not his favorite Islay distillery, but it would do, since he was in a mood for some peat flavor.

Max wore the expression of a man horribly defeated, emasculated, humiliated. How could he go back to Jimmy T. empty handed? Max rubbed the back of his neck and swiveled it from side to side to work the stress out. On the return trip from swiveling it to the right, his eyes met the man on his left. Max continued to work the kinks out of his neck.

Each time his head swung around to his neighbor he took in a few more details. Deep tan. Thin wispy hair combed over to hide baldness. Extremely skinny. Max glanced down and noticed an ancient brown leather case with two snap-down flaps sitting on the floor next to the man's ankle. Max stopped swinging his head. The tan man's eyes bugged out of their sockets.

After an eternity of frozen time, the lanky man grabbed the suitcase and bolted for the door. Max threw some money on the bar top and followed like a streaker in wintertime. Outside on the pavement he could spot the man's head bobbing up and down in the crowd. He tried to hang back so the man would be lulled into a false sense of security. The man ran down several twisty side streets and Max lost him after three turns.

Damn.

He had two options, either the alley on the left or straight ahead. Max chose the alley on the left. As he proceeded down it, he noticed the buildings grew closer together, angling in so it was harder for the sunlight to spill in. The light that managed to infiltrate the alley dribbled spots of pale yolk around the brick and stone. He heard birds twittering and looked up at the sound of footsteps on a fire escape, observing just in time a skinny ankle darting through an open window. As Max stepped onto the bottom rung of the fire escape he was conscious of the sound of a distant backfire interrupting the birds in their chirping. He clambered up the rest of the stairs and poked his head into the room.

His heart sunk. There, spread eagle on the floor, was the suitcase burglar. A thick, inky blotch of red had spread itself across his chest. An irreverent thought of strawberry syrup on pancakes popped into Max's head. He subconsciously noticed the smell of a discharged gun. Was the killer still in the room? With blood pumping through his heart at a ridiculous speed, Max slowly crawled the rest of the way into the room and quickly looked around with darting glances, expecting to be smacked on the head like James Garner on TV.

The suitcase was gone.

He stepped across the body, looking at it but trying not to, and went around the corner and found the front door to the room ajar. No one was in the hall, so he pushed the door closed with his knuckles and gave the room his full attention. He had to be quick, for he didn't know how long it would be before someone followed the sound of the gunshot.

A business card, a partial roll of breath mints, some toothpicks, and some change were on the dresser. The card read:

Reinhold Geiz

Barnard, Ganns, & Malcolms

Publishing House

1410 Fourth Ave. New York, N.Y.

Of course! Barnard, Ganns, and Malcolms was the original publisher of the Old Man's early work. His book sales singlehandedly made them an overnight sensation. In recent years their empire had begun to crumble, in fact Max had thought they were a defunct operation. Finding the lost manuscript would put them back on the map. But now it seemed someone wanted the book more than Reinhold Geiz.

Max decided the business card was the only clue he needed, as he was not going to rummage through the corpse's clothing and leave fingerprints and hair fibers around. Fleecing the room for more clues seemed the correct thing to do, but his heart was beating out of control, and he was developing a hyperventilation problem. He was starting to become very paranoid being in the room with a murdered man for that long. In an old 1950s movie the coppers would bust in, catching him red-handed at the scene of a crime he did not commit. Those foolish old Hollywood actors always hung around just a smidge too long. The stupidest character had to be Carey Grant in *North by Northwest*, taking the knife out of a dead man's back as a news photographer takes his picture.

His steps sounded very loud to him as he climbed down the fire escape. Looking around, he was certain no one saw him. In a moment of rare clear thinking, Max thought maybe he should go around to the front and see what hotel he had just escaped from, as the logo on the towels looked vaguely familiar.

Max couldn't believe it. It was the same hotel he was in an hour ago, asking about room 142. Reinhold Geiz, if the dead man was the owner of the card, must have checked out for some reason and then decided to check back in. Or he just sneaked back into his old room to escape Max.

Max went back to his own hotel and called Jimmy T. Blick.

"I'm coming back home. People are stealing and killing for that suitcase and I don't want any part of it."

"Now, boy, don't get yer garter belt all bunched up."

"My garter is just fine," Max stammered, "especially when you consider how close I've come to being murdered."

"Yer not going to be murdered, boy. Jus' git yer ass on over to London. There's someone in town who knows where the bag is." His speech was slurring, probably from the effects of expensive grain alcohol.

"How the hell is that possible, Jimmy, unless you know who the murderer is? *And* why go to London if the bag is here? Unless you know it is en route to London right now. The murderer has the bag, remember? And you said you have someone that knows where the bag is. Hmmmm."

Silence.

"Jimmy, there are only two ways you can know who the killer is: one, you initiated the murder yourself, or two, you have another person over here working on the job behind my back!"

Jimmy laughed. "Now, sugar, you never said we were seein' each other exclusive-like.

I've got lots of sweethearts all over. Jealous?"

Max didn't see the humor. Jimmy promised him no more danger would come his way and he was not involved in the murder. The rest of the adventure would be a cakewalk. Max should trust him and go to London and look up a Moris Tate.

"You can thank me later, boy."

3

After being stuck on a roundabout for five minutes, Max was finally able to navigate his little rental down the radiating street he needed. The streets were so tiny that he could see why the rental agency didn't offer Buicks or Lincolns. Max turned down Greyhound St. and found the hotel. The Paragon wasn't the fanciest hotel in the world, but it was a lot nicer than he was used to. It was a skyscraper, or looked like one in comparison to its surroundings, not far from Earl's Court, and it looked to have been built in maybe the '70s, judging by the architecture. It was probably a big deal to the corporate traveler back in its heyday. He walked through the double doors and asked the cute French girl behind the desk to call up Moris Tate.

"She will meet you in the bar," the girl said as she hung up the phone.

She?

Max got directions to the bar and ambled along the corridor slowly. This could be promising, Max thought. Maybe she would be attractive. So what if she had a stodgy old man's name? He ordered some Benedictine and brandy, just to change his usual routine, and waited with anticipation for Moris.

A chunky fifty-some-odd-year-old woman in an ill-fitting lavender suit walked in. Her short gray hair was tightly coiled in waxen circles, probably just having been released from curler bondage. The giant cravat-like bow on her blouse concealed most of her double chin. As she approached Max he rose to meet her, but she continued on past him. With an exhale of relief he sat back onto his stool.

Max had another theory, known to his friends as "The Secret Label." This theory stated that we all have a label that people use to describe us to others but that we are not aware of. Ever wonder how a different waitress from the one you gave your order to delivers your food directly to you and not to one of your dinner partners? Simple. The Secret Label. At shift change the one waitress says to the other, "The bald man gets the ravioli, the lady with the mustache to his left has the soup, and the pasty skinny guy gets the steak." How does the front desk clerk at a hotel pick you out of a crowded lobby to tell you that you have a phone call? The Secret Label. The caller tells the hotel operator to give a message to the chubby wall-eyed guy. We all have a secret label, some more attractive than others, just as their namesakes are. Max hoped that Moris had a desirable label. A name-brand label.

The stool next to Max made a scraping sound as it was dragged out to allow room for a patron's ample bottom. She was exaggeratedly pear shaped with a head of frazzled dyed-brown hair, and, as Max judged, was a poorly aged fifty with a striking resemblance to Clint Eastwood in his later years. She wore a brown wool skirt suit that probably cost a fortune back in 1974, and a gold chain around her neck bore a marble cameo of what appeared to be a profile of Cloris Leachman. But the thing most important to Max's observations was the dog-eared book she was carrying in her handbag. It was one of the Old Man's early classics. Kind of an obvious way to identify one's self on this mission, Max thought.

"You, uh, like him?" Max said to the woman, indicating the book with his eyebrows.

The woman looked down to where Max's glance led. "Oh, yes," she said with a heavy Irish accent. "I usually only read him in the spring, as he reminds me of Africa."

Oh, this is too much, Max thought. This is getting silly. Are we acting out a ridiculous spy scenario, now? We have code words, do we? Looking straight ahead into the bar mirror, Max said, "Yes, but the ice is slippery in the summertime."

The woman regarded him as if he were a koala bear that had just sung a medley of Smokey Robinson tunes.

"The fat man walks alone?" he continued, talking out of the side of his mouth.

"Sir," she said, "I think you have had enough to drink." And with that she took her handbag and relocated herself to the far end of the bar.

Nine uncomfortable minutes passed, and then, as Max was consulting his watch, trying to avoid the stare of the lady in the wool suit, he heard a young voice behind him ask, "Are you Max?"

When Max turned to greet her, he silently thanked his maker.

And her maker, too, for Moris was in her mid-twenties, with shoulder-length dark brown and strawberry-accented hair, a preference for incredibly tight clothing, and a strong resemblance to the number eight. The curvy number folded herself in two and perched on the stool next to him.

Max opened the conversation with: "Guwnn."

"I'm sorry?" Moris replied.

"Excuse me. That was my best opening line."

She blinked at him, not comprehending his attempt at levity, and his weak attempt at recovery. Max explained:

"I'm sorry. To be honest I was expecting a man."

"Yes, so was I," Moris answered while lighting her cigarette.

"Oh, good. For a moment I thought we were going to get off on the wrong foot, there." He tried a charming smile.

"Look, we're here for one purpose, Max, and that is to get the suitcase. If you are not on board I suggest you don't waste our time, and get off."

"…before the ship sinks?" Max suggested.

She rolled her eyes and blew out smoke.

"Look," Max oozed, "why don't we go back to your room and discuss this like two mature adults that enjoy taking baths together?"

Moris again rolled her eyes aggressively, snatched up her lighter, slid off the stool, and twitched on out of the hotel pub.

Max was disappointed at losing his chance at a happy one-night relationship, but at the same time pleased that he had gotten himself out of finishing the assignment. He walked back to the reception counter, remembering that there was an attractive little French girl at the desk. Perhaps the evening wouldn't be a total loss.

Instead, "Brad" stood there, alone, behind the reception desk with his smug little crooked nametag.

"A room for one?" Brad chirped.

"YES!" Max growled.

The door swung into the bed corner of his corporate shoebox room, so Max could barely finagle himself and his Samsonite inside. Crap. His dead-end job was looking more and more attractive to him. Throwing himself down on the bed like a fish on a dock, he turned on the pint-sized TV and surfed the five channels. An old repeat of *Cheers*, a talk show about knitting, heavily edited porn, Sumo wrestling, and…

The phone rang. He let it ring for quite a while before picking it up.

"Hey, this is Moris. Look, I talked to Jimmy T. and he feels, for some reason, that it is important that we work…together." She tried to sound pleasant but it was obviously killing her.

"I'm having a hard time hearing you. Why don't you come up to my room?" Max nearly sang.

"I will not come up to your room."

"What's that, Moris? You're break-ing u-p. I c-an barely hear y-" Click. Max hung up with a smile.

A minute passed and the telephone rang again. A cold, tightly controlled, feminine voice said: "What room are you in? The desk says they aren't allowed to give out room numbers."

"519. Bring some bubble bath."

......

Max knew she was using him and was only doing what Jimmy T. had ordered her to do, but Max seldom had a chance to spend a night with a woman so far out of his league. Frankly, he didn't care. He had a grand time.

"So now that you've sated your appetite," she tugged the sheet she had coiled herself in closer to her neck, "can we get down to business?"

"Again, Moris? You're insatiable."

"Not that kind of business, Max, and you know it." She lit a cigarette like she'd been doing it since she was seven. As gossamer swirls of shifting grey floated to the ceiling, she studied the tip of the flame in order to avoid eye contact with Max.

"Will you be honest with me and explain how you know where the suitcase is when it was stolen by a murderer?"

"Sure." She got up, making sure that all of her flesh was concealed in the tightly wrapped bed sheet, and crossed to the bathroom. The shower water ran for twenty minutes or so, then she reemerged, wet and tightly wrapped in a white towel.

She busied herself with starting another cigarette, emptying the ashtray, arranging the magazines and hotel literature.

"Are you done redecorating? I thought you wanted to get down to business," Max flippantly remarked in what he imagined was his best Bogart monotone.

"What was the question again?"

Max stood up and grabbed her tightly by the towel. Staring deliberately into her eyes, he asked, "Did you or didn't you kill that Geiz publisher for the suitcase?"

"I didn't." Moris looked like she would stab him if she only had a knife. "But I *will* kill you."

"Answer my questions first." Max said, pulling tighter on the towel. "If you didn't, then who did?"

"I think it was a rival publisher."

"Name."

"Antoine Starv. I was…attaching myself to him, gaining his confidence. All of a sudden he had the suitcase, so I can only assume that he's the one that shot him."

"How do you know that it was a shot that killed him?" Max barked at her.

She was silent for a moment, then: "Jimmy told me. You told Jimmy, remember?"

The girl was lying somewhere, Max just wasn't sure where. Maybe she pulled the trigger, or perhaps it was this Antoine Starv person. He couldn't tell. He was almost certain, however, that when she said she "attached" herself to him she meant that she was sleeping with Starv, just as she had slept with Max to get what she needed—his cooperation. He just had to bide his time and see if he could make her slip up, all the while watching his own back.

"So," Max began, "if Starv ended up with the suitcase, how come you didn't run with it?"

"Because I think he got wise to me. He disappeared."

"I'm glad to see that I'm not the only one that sucks at his job," Max remarked with a little venom.

Moris pulled her body away from Max's grip, carefully so the towel wouldn't drop, moved around him, making sure her figure was covered in all the important places, and walked into the bathroom, closing the door behind her.

"What's our next move then?" Max asked loudly through the door. He rested his head against the doorframe. "He could be anywhere."

She cracked the door. "Hand me my clothes."

Max dutifully passed the garments through the slender space that she allotted for the transfer. A couple minutes passed with no rebuttal, and then she made her exit from the bath, dressed and looking as fresh as she had when she had originally arrived.

"After he vanished I asked the reception desk at his hotel for a copy of the bill. They had seen us together so much that they assumed we were a couple. " Max smelled a stretching of the truth. He surmised that they probably did indeed share the same room in unmarried sin. "Starv had made two phone calls to Spain and then the last call was to Iberian airlines. He's in Toledo."

"Ohio?"

"Spain. We have tickets for a flight that leaves in four hours. And I'm taking a nap," she added coolly, clearly still angry. She let herself out.

4

Max could see she was not going to defrost. Moris only spoke when she absolutely needed to, so Max contented himself by drinking whiskey the entire flight. She wasn't any better in the rental car as they made their trek to Toledo from Madrid. They had rented a Citroen Picasso. Another family trying to suck all the money out of a famous name, Max thought angrily. Moris insisted that she be the driver and he the map reader. She never needed to consult the map.

With nothing to do, Max's mind drifted off to the carnal encounter he had shared earlier with this beautiful young chauffer. He often wondered over the years why he had this character flaw, this need for women, plural, instead of a need for a woman, singular. At this late point in his life he should be growing roots and settling down with one person. It obviously must have had something to do with his father abandoning the family and then getting himself killed, but his alcoholic mother must've contributed to Dad's insanity. She probably drove him to other women. For years he thought his father just up and left. It wasn't till his teen years that he discovered the truth, while looking through some papers he found in his mother's closet. There were letters and several newspaper clippings. He pieced the story together with the evidence at hand.

His father was having an affair with a married neighbor down the street. He left Max's mother, probably thinking the girl would do the same on her end, but she didn't; she stayed with her man. Dad soon found out he had cancer, and rather than face that horror, deliberately got himself shot by his mistress's jealous husband. It had to be deliberate. The witnesses interviewed in the papers said he seemed to be bating the angry husband, daring him to pull the trigger. The man gave his father two favors: he loaned him his wife and put him out of his misery.

Max suspected that there were also affairs on his mother's part. He had bizarre childhood memories and whenever he had, as a young adult, asked his mother about them, she'd insist that they were merely fragments of dreams that his imagination had conjured up. Max bought that for a while, but eventually came to understand that she was lying to him.

His strangest "dream" was spending a night in a small laundry room when he was five or so. Mom had taken him to a new friend's house. Her "friend" was considerably older

than his own father; this man was in his late
fifties, heavy with fatty old muscle, and with
a head of slicked-back steel-grey hair.

His mother had always been a social
climber, a pilot fish, as he recalled a high
school sociology teacher calling it, and she
went where the fame or fortune lay. This male
friend of hers was a business man that had
once played professional baseball, and was, at
the time of this memory, running for some
political position.

The evening at the man's house stretched
long until it became late, and Max, like five-
year-olds can get, was cranky and tired and
wanted to go home, but every time he asked,
his mother would say no. He had already
explored the big house, and the excitement of
the newness of it had worn off. He sensed that
he was annoying her and she wished that he
wasn't there. Finally she said that it was so

late that it wasn't safe to drive. They would stay the night there at the man's house.

The older man, with his bulbous glass of wine in hand, showed Max to a very small dark room that contained a cot, already made up, and a washing machine and dryer. Max was horrified but did not want to show the man that he was frightened. His mother claimed she would be sleeping on the couch, but later his ears told him that she was in the man's bedroom all night, laughing drunkenly.

The next morning Max found his mother in the kitchen drinking champagne and orange juice. He asked where the man was and she pointed out to the panoramic view of the ocean. Behind the wall of glass was a huge expanse of blue that went on infinitely.

She said, "He's swimming. He swims five miles every morning."

Max couldn't believe it. What kind of a super man could swim that far out, out to the horizon probably, and with sharks and giant squid all around?

At that moment the man came back in, dripping wet, with matted grey hair all over his chest like some kind of a yeti. He scared Max, yet impressed him.

Will I grow up to be this cool, Max thought?

A caravan of tall, slender buses passed the rented Citroen, snapping Max out of his reverie. He was back in the present—back in a passenger seat and being driven by a beautiful woman in a foreign land. Maybe he *did* grow up to be as cool as his mother's lover with the beach house.

It seemed like an eternity before they finally saw the medieval city perched up on the hillside. Branches of white light streaked down from between clouds and hit ancient buildings with sharp angular highlights. Their little car wound its way up a tiny street into the town and they stopped at the first hotel they came to. It looked nice and clean, with various flags jutting out from the front of the portico, but it was in a very dark alley. Light seldom found its way down into that labyrinth. The entire front of the lobby entrance was a wall of glass panes with a revolving door in the center. The childish side of Max always loved revolving doors. He took it easy on Moris, resisting the temptation to jump in with her, and let her go through it alone.

Inside, as they approached the blonde wood desk, Max opened his mouth to ask the blonde behind it for a double room, but Moris beat him to the punch, asking for two single rooms. When the Spanish girl said she was having a hard time finding two adjacent, Moris eagerly volunteered to have her room on another floor. Keys for #213 and #313 were issued.

"Would you like to be on top?" Max inquired of Moris, dangling the key for #313. There was no response to his innuendo and she plucked the key from his hand like a viper.

Max passed his floor and continued on up the staircase with Moris to her floor. She shot him a cold glance. Smiling, he walked her to her door and saw her safely in. He stuck his head in the door and looked around.

"Mmm, nice." There was a double bed with no foot- or headboard. On the wall hung a sun-bleached print of El Greco's portrayal of Toledo in its glamour days. She was given one spindly nightstand and a crooked yellow lamp circa 1970.

"I'll meet you in, say, twenty minutes?" Max inquired.

"In the lobby!" she said, positioning her bag in front of her and deliberately not looking at Max. She was not big on eye contact.

Max trotted down the steps to his room whistling "Don't Sit under the Apple Tree with Anyone Else but Me." Inside, his was a similar arrangement to Moris's room, except the print was replaced with a needlepoint rendition of a cathedral. He opened his window and a moment later heard the window from the room above him creak open.

Day dreaming, he found himself wondering if it was Moris who opened the window above. Hers was room 313 and his 213, so numerically it made sense that she was directly above, but who knew if the building was laid out like that. If it was, he could play Romeo and scale the creepers up to her room. It wasn't a family name, though, that kept them apart, but Moris herself. And his fear of heights.

There was nothing in the room to help him pass the time. His Spanish wasn't good enough to follow the programs on TV, so he went downstairs to hang out in the lobby. Morris came down ten minutes late.

"What's our plan of attack?" Max asked.

"Well, it's a small town; if we just look long enough we're bound to run into Starv."

"Seriously? That's your plan?"

"Hey," Moris said defensively, "I got you this far. We really don't have any other options."

"Fine. Where shall we start?"

"We should split up. That way we have a better chance of spotting him."

"I have no idea what this guy looks like," Max exclaimed.

"I'll describe him to you."

"It's not the same. You can spot him instantly since you know him, whereas I could look right through him in a crowd of people. Or worse yet, waste my time following someone I think is him but isn't."

She saw Max's point but wanted him to try it her way first.

Antoine Starv was in his late thirties with a medium build. His hair was entirely white like an old man's. He had a pasty pale complexion and wasn't really ugly or handsome, but lingered somewhere in between. Except for the white hair he sounded like a very unnoticeable person.

They parted company, Moris turning to the right out the lobby doors, and Max turning left. Max quickly stepped into an alley and stood in the shadows, watching Moris make her way down the street. As soon as he felt she was far enough ahead of him, he stepped out onto the cobblestones and followed her at a distance. After a while Moris quickly looked back over her shoulder. Fortunately for Max he had just bent down to tie his loose shoelace. He backed off and tried to stay behind clusters of people. She checked behind her again and then darted into a hotel. Max cautiously peeked into the lowest pane of glass, obscured by a potted palm inside, and saw Moris entering a small cage elevator. He couldn't enter the lobby since she would spot him through the bars of the cage. He watched the elevator rise.

As soon as the elevator stopped, Max ran into the lobby and checked the floor numbers on the display to figure out which one she got off on, and made a mad dash for the stairs. He arrived on the fourth floor, out of breath, dizzy, and a little shaky from the excitement of the chase. Trying to look casual, Max hovered around doors hoping to pick up Moris' voice.

After listening to almost every door a couple of times, a hotel maid came out of a closet and walked up behind him. His ear was pressed flush up against a door when he realized someone was standing behind him. Spinning around and stammering, Max searched his memory banks, perusing his limited Spanish vocabulary for words that might explain his behavior. All he could think to do was rub the spot on the door where his ear had been and point. He eventually gave up and bolted down the stairs, leaving a perplexed housekeeper with the idea that Americans are all crazy.

Out on the pavement Max collected himself and tried to plan a strategy. He could sit in the lobby and wait for her to come down. He would love to see the look on her face when she saw him, but that could ruin everything. Most certainly she was seeing Starv; he just wished he could be sure. Suddenly getting an idea, he ran back inside.

"May I speak with Antoine Starv?" he asked the clerk behind the counter.

The clerk fumbled with the computer for a moment before stating in excellent English that no one by that name was in house.

Well, Max thought, that didn't mean he wasn't staying there. He had used many an alias himself when staying in hotels with other people's spouses and daughters. Maybe he should let Moris carry on with her charade and see where it might lead.

Max went three doors down to a little restaurant and ordered dinner on the outside patio. He figured Moris would probably pass by him on her way back and he could pull a "Fancy meeting you here…"

The restaurant's patio was a small brick patch on the sidewalk, with two tables, fenced in with a railing to keep the drunken pedestrians from falling into the laps of diners. Max took a chair that faced the direction Moris would be coming from.

To stretch out his dining experience so that it would last till she came by, he decided to start with cocktails. After he nursed a couple drinks, he had a salad, and when the main course arrived, so did the delectable Miss Moris.

"Ah, dessert came a little early," Max called out.

She was trying not to see him so her act of surprise would look more natural.

"Moris Tate. Fancy meetin' you here. What a small world."

"No luck yet?" She leaned unconsciously in a provocative manner against the rickety wrought-iron rail that had probably been there since El Cid came to town.

She looked lovely. Bright sunlight low in the sky showed through gaps between the buildings and then gaps between strands of Moris' hair. Her complexion was as clear as a child's, and there was a faint sprinkling of freckles across her cheeks and chest. Her straight arm on the rail drove her shoulder up to her ear. Her hip jutted out in a contrapposto stance, accentuating her curves.

Moments like this were the reason Max found himself so often in trouble with women. As a womanizer he could be labeled as a woman hater, also because he treated them as hunted game and seemed to have very little respect for the gender. However, he would argue that he loved them all in his own way. He loved their individual laughs, their hand and head movements, their personalities, the way they expressed themselves, the little details of how a woman may push unwanted hair out of her eye by carefully wrapping it behind her ear, or how she may tilt her head to the side when something is confusing, or bite her lower lip when concentrating, and all of the other little nuances that make women so very different from men.

Still admiring her, he answered her question. "No. No luck. Have you eaten yet?" Before she could answer he told her, "Take a seat. I recommend the corn dogs."

"Very funny, Max." She almost sounded friendly when she said it, like there were the beginnings of a hidden laugh behind her tone. She came around the rail and took the other chair.

Max knew that Moris felt as though she were in the hot seat and had to play nice. People always do that when they are almost caught red handed. They overcompensate with kindness so as to not raise suspicion about what they were just doing. Max had seen it a thousand times. Years of training and close calls had taught Max how not to react in that way, and Moris was definitely overcompensating. Maybe he could overcompensate Moris back into bed again. With practiced ease, he began to manipulate the conversation.

"Have you picked up any clues yet?" he asked.

"No, not really. I've been asking around."

"Where?" Max pried. "I don't want to overlap and start asking questions in places where you've already been."

That made her squirm. She pretended to get distracted by a piece of dirty silverware that she had discovered, buying time to collect her thoughts and come up with an answer.

"Oh, let's see, I did all down this street and the one up to the right."

"All of the businesses?"

"No, just the hotels and bars," Moris mumbled. "I need a menu."

Max waved down a waiter and got her a menu. Her food soon arrived and Moris struggled to keep the conversation light. Max took full advantage of having her backed into a corner and enjoyed the pleasant date-like conversation.

"You know, I'm not such a bad guy. If we had met under different circumstances we might be friends."

"I don't think you're a bad guy."

"You know what I mean, Moris. It's this whole crazy adventure. I don't usually conduct myself like this. I have a quiet little job in the US and am not used to running down alleys after murderers. Throw a mysterious and beautiful woman whose intentions are dubious into the mix, and I start acting like James Bond, extorting women so they sleep with me."

Moris silently chased lettuce around her plate and then worked on constructing a wall against Max with the rice from her paella. She kept sliding her fork toward him, pushing and fortifying her wall of yellow rice, keeping him at bay.

"Now can you really blame me, Moris? I mean, look at you. You are so far out of my league I would normally never have a chance to date someone like you."

"You do have a point."

"What?" Max gasped. "Was that an attempt at humor?"

"I have my moments."

"Now see, this is so much nicer than the cold shoulder."

He smiled. One of Max's odd habits was casting people as if life was his own special movie. Not everyone bore a strong resemblance to someone famous, but there were definite types. Max felt Moris would be played by an old B-list movie starlet from the '50s named Martha Hyer. She had a similar type of beauty.

Max proceeded cautiously, since he didn't want to screw up the pleasant moment they were sharing.

"So now that you know I'm not normally a bad guy, can you share a little bit about yourself? Who is Moris Tate? I know this cool, tough facade can't be all there is to you."

"I like to macramé and needlepoint."

"Are you serious?" Max laughed.

"No."

"Ay-yi-yi, I'm getting nowhere with this woman. Can you at least tell me a favorite color? What song did you dance to at your prom? What kind of tree would you be? If you were elected Miss America how would you stamp out world peace?"

"Oh please." She tried to repress a smile. "Stop it, Max."

"Which do you prefer? Beatles or Stones? Folgers or Sanka?"

"Oh, God."

"Do you stick Q-tips in your ear or follow doctor's orders and use a wash cloth? Pancakes or waffles? Aquaman or Submariner? Dr. Pepper or Mr. Pibb?"

"Stop it!" Moris laughed.

"Linkin Logs or Tinker Toys?"

"You've got to run out soon."

"No, I can go on like this all day. *Little House on the Prairie* or *Highway to*

Heaven? Scrambled or fried? When parking on level ground, do you use your emergency brake?"

"No more. You're killing me!"

Max laughed, "Okay, last one. Which leg do you shave first in the morning? No! Wait, one more! Which would you rather be in a carnival freak show—the bearded lady or the goat girl?"

He finally gave up and they enjoyed a period of silence as their mirth died down. Moris took a drink of her wine and breathed deeply.

"Okay," she began, "I was born in Oklahoma, went to college in Vermont, majored in political science, worked in the school bookstore and a shopping mall jewelry store."

"Fascinating," Max mocked. "No, tell me good stuff. First boyfriend. Stuff like that, and funny stories, too."

"Okay, let me think." She bit the corner of her mouth. "Okay, here's one. We went—my boyfriend and I—we went with some other couples camping. There were four or five couples and I was friends with all the girls. They were in my dorm on my floor. We didn't bring tents; we were all going to sleep out under the stars in sleeping bags. Well, everyone starts drinking and soon some of the couples are fooling around in their sleeping bags, not being very discrete as to what they're doing."

"And you were a good girl?"

"Oh yes. In those days, yes. So, soon everyone starts passing out and dropping off one by one because we are just hammered. I'm surprised none of us died from alcohol poisoning that night. Anyway, then in the middle of the night I shoot up wide awake and I can't go back to sleep. Bear in mind, I am still drunk out of my mind. I have this strange tendency when I drink to get a wanderlust and I often go exploring. Always with bad results. So I crawl out of my bag and decide to go walk in the woods. I'm wandering around in the woods wearing nothing but my underwear and this little shirt thing—"

"Wait," Max interrupted. "Talk slower."

"Oh stop, you pervert. So I'm out there, wandering around in the woods, extremely intoxicated and extremely lost. Right when I start to get a little panicky because I'm all turned around and don't think I can find my way back, I come upon a boy. He's my age and he says he is lost, too, and *he* is obviously very drunk. Can't find his way back to his campsite either."

Max laughed.

"What are the odds? Two people from different parties lost, and they find each other!"

"Wow, that's great," Max marveled, thoroughly enjoying her story.

"So we decided to join forces and team up."

"Very logical."

"Yes, I thought so. Eventually after an hour or more of wandering around, we see these headlights coming through the trees and it's a forest ranger. He picked us up and drove us around to various sites to see if any of them were our friends. We found mine first. And guess what."

"What?"

"In the morning no one believed me that I got up and went on an adventure. They all told me I dreamed it."

"Even your boyfriend?"

"Even my boyfriend. Who quickly became my ex-boyfriend."

"Good. Drop the dead wood. Who needs him," Max approved. "I have a drunken story, too. Actually, I have too many drunken stories, but we'll start with this one. I was dating this girl and we fell on hard luck. We were very young and I had just lost my job so we had to move in with the girl's mother————she took us in, which was nice, but as you can imagine, very awkward. We had our own room, at least, so there was some privacy. One night I was out drinking with the boys and came staggering home when the bar closed and kicked me out. So, I make the walk home somehow and stagger into my room and, with great difficulty, get out of my pants and pass out on the bed. In the morning I wake up and feel something hairy lying next to me."

"Oh no," Moris interjected.

"Just wait. Now, hurting from the hangover, I open one eye to see what it is. The dog is in bed with me. But the dog isn't allowed in Shelley's room. Strange, I think to myself. It always sleeps with her mother."

"Oh no!"

"Right!" Max clapped his hands. "I see over the dog's body this woman's head slowly start to rise and peer at me. 'Max?' she said."

"You slept in her mother's bed?"

"I had slept the whole night with my girlfriend's mother! I had staggered into the wrong room. And now I'm there with my pants off."

"I hope you didn't, you know…"

"With the mother or the dog?"

They finished dinner and walked back to their hotel, chatting pleasantly. Max could see that the conversation was winding down and he was going to get a parting handshake from her and they would go their separate ways as platonic friends. He needed to make Moris nervous about being caught in a lie and get her to overcompensate.

"You know," Max said craftily, stopping at the elevator, "I think I did get a glimpse of someone meeting Starv's description, but I lost him. I think he ducked into a hotel that was a few doors down from where we had dinner. I ate there so I could hang around and see if I could get another look at him. If you're going to bed, maybe I'll go on back and loiter around that hotel for a while."

"No." Moris grabbed his shirtfront. "Why don't you come up to my room for a drink? We'll start again fresh tomorrow."

Max, you truly are a bastard, he thought to himself.

......

Max silently let himself out of Moris's room and trotted down the steps, lightly whistling the theme song to *Peter Gunn*. Fishing the room key out of his pocket, he reflected on what a great evening it had turned out to be. The ample charms of Moris had made the trip almost worthwhile. Too bad she was lying and deceptive. He could imagine settling down with someone like her.

Max took a quick shower and went to bed with sugarplum fairies dancing in his head. He was right on the brink of sleep when all of a sudden he got his second wind and was wide away. He hated that. It was always like that when there was a lot of excitement in his life. He'd be exhausted from the adventure, but then adrenalin would kick in and he couldn't stop his thoughts from racing.

The thought of settling down with Moris triggered the memory of his one and only attempt at the revered tradition of matrimony. The marriage was brief, only lasting three months, because Max was caught in bed with a Denny's waitress. Fortunately his wife didn't know about the nurse, the Macy's store clerk, and the veterinarian that came before the waitress. Max got married because he thought that is what boys and girls do. Now he understood that there are certain types of people that are not meant to enter that institution.

That's not exactly true. It was his first relationship *after* the marriage that taught him that lesson.

Her name was Nan and she hated her name passionately. She hated the full version,

Nanna, even more. She said it was the name of the dog that the kids dressed as a maid in Peter Pan, and also what children called their grandmothers. Max was amused and thought her allusion true, but, nonetheless, grew to love the name as he grew to love her. He was the only one she'd allow to call her by her full name.

Love eluded Max his entire life, but when Nanna found him so did love, and it grabbed him hard. A year and a half went by and Max never cheated on her, never even thought of it, and had no other desire but for her. He loved spending time with her, in and out of bed. Where it was easy to make most women laugh, it was a challenge with Nanna, probably because she saw through his thick veneer of bullshit. They had several things in common, but not everything. The best thing they had in common were their personalities. They meshed like the teeth on gears, snuggly rotating together.

The couple was inseparable. They'd even lunch together every day at a restaurant between their two places of work. They'd talk about books, art, and movies, exchanging their favorite novels with the other to read. There were never any of the usual mind games one finds at the beginning of a relationship, and jealousy simply didn't exist. They made one another feel so secure in their love that there was no need for the word jealousy in their vocabulary. One day Max had even commented on it to her.

"When I was a teenager I saw Dasheille Hammett's movie, *The Thin Man*. Seen it?" She had. "Well, there's this scene where this beautiful girl breaks down crying on Nick's chest, so he puts his arm around her and pats her on the back to console her. In walks his wife, Nora. So you instantly get tense, thinking there's going to be this big misunderstanding where Nora thinks he's cheating on her. Instead, over the girl's shoulder, Nick makes the 'husband face' at Nora, which says: Get the hell out of here, you're interrupting. She nods her head and DOES. I remember thinking at the time—now remember, I'm a teenager with not much experience with women behind me—and I thought that Nora's behavior was extremely unusual. A woman walks in and her husband is hugging a young gorgeous girl, but she is so secure in the knowledge that her husband loves her, she doesn't for a moment think anything untoward is happening, doesn't jump to conclusions, because she knows so thoroughly that infidelity isn't even an option. I loved that and thought that I would grow up and have a relationship just like that. Loyal best friends."

He had finally found it with Nanna. She agreed, and Max shared his theory about what people often mistake for love. He had noticed in prior relationships that women did not fall in love with him but fell in love with how he made them feel. He made them laugh, he was romantic and charming and heaped compliments on them, but eventually he realized, they loved the warm fuzzy feeling he gave them and the boost of self esteem they got from being with him, but when it came right down to it, it wasn't *him* they loved. They loved that he made them love themselves. Nanna assured Max that that was not the case with her. It was the happiest time in Max's young life.

Then one day she disappeared. Max didn't worry too much, as she was prone to disappearing for short periods without calling. Being an introspective person, she needed a great deal of time alone, which Max tried to be understanding about. In the beginning he found it odd, but after a year and a half of her occasional disappearances, he became used to it. Plus, she made him feel just as secure as he did her. In fact, the last conversation they had had ended with her saying he was the only man she could ever see herself being with.

When a week turned into two, Max began to get more than a little nervous. He didn't want to bombard her voicemail with tons of messages, yet he wanted to know if she was alright. He left a few concerned messages and then forced himself to stop. By the third week he was frantic. Why was she doing this? What had he done wrong? Everything was perfect between them, she had said so just before she dropped out. He kept himself from going by her apartment. He didn't want to appear like a stalker, yet he was getting so scared he had to do something. Suppose she had died a week ago and he didn't know?

He had stopped eating and was sick with worry. At the beginning of the fourth week he decided he had to go by her place. That evening Max drove by her place slowly, fearful that she'd pop her head out her window and see him creeping by. Her car was gone but the condo didn't look abandoned. There wasn't a pile of rolled newspapers left on the doorstep. That meant she was still alive, at least. But what if she had been in an accident and her mother was coming by every day, watering plants, picking up mail and papers?

The next day Max went by her work and her car wasn't there. He knew if he went into the shop they wouldn't tell him when she worked next, as they had no idea who he was. The world was a cautious place now, and employers didn't hand out their employees' schedules to anyone off the street. He figured he'd go in and play it by ear.

Approaching a pretty girl with darkish blonde hair he asked, "Hey, is Samantha…No, that doesn't sound right. Nanna? Do you have a woman named Nanna working today?"

"Oh, you must mean Nan," she volunteered.

"That's right. That's it—Nan," Max said, pointing at her as if she hit the nail right on the head.

"No, she's off today."

"Oh. She was a terrific help to me the other day and I feel I must have been a real nuisance, so I'd like to give her a tip. I understand you probably aren't allowed to tell me…"

"You can leave it with me if you like."

"I could, but I really wanted to thank her personally and apologize for being so difficult."

"You can come by tomorrow after three. She should be in by then."

"Thank you. I think I'll try."

The next day at three he met Nanna as she was getting out of her car. He felt he probably looked like one of those crazed maniacs that women take restraining orders out against. The look of pale fear on Nanna's face ground the impression further into his conscience. She froze, half in and half out of the car. Her eyes were huge and unblinking. Max knew in that instant that his fears were true. She had left him and never bothered to tell him.

"Really, Nanna? This is how you were going to do it? Just disappear...never have the decency to tell me to my face, give me any kind of closure?"

She didn't say anything, but just stared with that look of an animal frozen by a car's headlights. Her face was white like fresh snow, her hair a disaster, and not a single stroke of makeup could be found on her face. The freckles on the bridge of her nose that he had always loved so much stood out sharply without a foundation powder to mute their color. Her lips were severely chapped. The cold wind which had suddenly kicked up blew her long hair across her face, dark strands sticking in her mouth.

"Don't be scared. I'm not the type to make a scene at your work. I love you, remember? I wouldn't do anything to hurt you."

She finally stirred and came out of the car the rest of the way. Closing the door, she leaned against it.

"Why?" He felt his voice begin to shake and loathed himself for the weakness.

"I don't know."

"You don't know? I think that sentence explains everything. My worst fears are true…" Still no response from her, just the cold wind moving hair across her face like little snakes. "You were The One. You said I was The One for you. We were planning a life together, Nanna. In fact, the last time I saw you, you said you couldn't imagine spending your life with any other man."

"I know." She looked down at her feet with dry eyes. Here I am struggling not to cry, he thought, and she can't even muster up one tear.

"So what is this? What have I done?"

"Nothing."

"You don't love me."

"That's not true."

"No? It's not? I think the evidence is on my side, Nana!" He wanted her to contradict him. Tell him it was all untrue and they'd go right back to being how they were. Instead, there was silence and no reassuring words. He was a little boy lost in an airport again, waiting for words of encouragement over a phone line.

"Do you think I would have left you miserable, left you hanging and confused for one hour, let alone a month, like you did me?" He was struggling now to not let tears well up in his eyes.

"No."

"Of course not. I would never do that to you. Do you know why? Because I love you. But you had no problem leaving me dangling and hurting."

Again, a painful silence. Then she finally spoke.

"It's just that my ex—"

"Oh, great."

"No, it's not like that—"

"You love him. Not me."

"No, it's not like that."

"Oh, really?" He couldn't control himself and started to raise his voice. "Is it me you're coming home to tonight or him? I think that means you love him, not me."

"It's not like that. It's just…well, he can help with my mortgage and pay for my school. We've worked out an arrangement."

"How romantic for you. I wish you the best." He turned to leave and then stopped, as if he couldn't let the moment pass. He knew he was dragging it out because this would be the last he ever saw of her. Finally, after a long moment of looking at her, cherishing her in a way she must have always taken for granted and never returned, he mumbled: "So many wasted words…" And then he quickly got in his car before he cried in front of her.

5

The next day was very uneventful for Max
and Moris. Max began his day by showering. His
memories from the night left him feeling like
he had a hangover. A tortured night like that,
a night of self-pity, hadn't broken through
his coconut shell hide in a long time. After
Nana he had developed a new philosophy. He
would use women for what he wanted, since they
used him for whatever it was they wanted him
for. The entire myth of romantic love, for
Max, was an exercise of popping holes in an
already deflated balloon. No one loved him and
he loved no one. People loved themselves and
indulged their cravings. Love is only a
fleeting chemical reaction in the brain.
Science would back him up on that one. The
Arthurian legends about a magical "one true

love" are just that—legends. In real life there are hundreds of one true loves. One leaves you, you find another. One gets hit by a car, you find another. He came to think of love as a disposable commodity, just like everything else in modern society. Max had no doubts about his philosophical slant on love—except on rare nights like the previous one. Fortunately, he knew how to keep those nights down to a minimum.

After a good scrubbing, some toothpaste, and mouthwash, Max was starting to feel like his old scoundrel self again. When he came down to the lobby and had an eye full of Moris in her beige pants that looked to have been brushed on with shellac, he truly began to feel like his self again.

"I didn't know you were a fan of decoupage," he said, eyeing her legs.

"What?"

"Never mind. Shall we commence our search? Lay on, MacDuff!"

"It's 'Lead on, MacDuff,'" Moris corrected.

"No, actually it's a common misquote. It's 'Lay on.' I remember my high school Shakespeare very well. It's kind of like 'Play it again, Sam.'"

"What? You're saying Bogart didn't say that?" She looked incredulous.

"That's what my lips are forming into words and projecting at you. Yes, he did not say that. Watch it when you get home if you don't believe me."

She gave him a look as if she couldn't tell which end of him the crazy started at and which end the madness finished.

The two stepped out onto the cobblestones and into a beautifully crisp blue day. The buildings' grey antique shadows crisscrossed the alleys and slithered merrily across their faces as they walked. They wandered aimlessly about the town together looking for Starv and the suitcase, or rather pretending to look for Starv and the suitcase. What was Moris's game? Max pondered the question from every angle, like a word search game in a children's magazine.

They took in the sights, saw the cathedral, looked at the bridge, and walked through the temple. They shared all three meals together, but it wasn't the same as the night before where they seemed to be making friends. At the end of the day Moris clearly drew the line in the sand, forbidding Max to cross it.

"I feel under the weather. I'm turning in early. Goodnight."

And that was it. Max was left to his own devices. As she turned and swished away in painted-on slacks, he felt a little hurt, a little disappointed, but it was expected. It wasn't like he thought they were going to become roommates, for he knew that Moris's affections were only available at a price. So, to pass time, he aimlessly bar-hopped, sampling various whiskeys and looking at the beautiful women Spain had to offer. He also tried to sort things out in his head.

They were trying to find a man named Antoine Starv who, according to Moris, had murdered a gent by the name of Reinhold Geiz, for the suitcase containing the Old Man's manuscript. Moris had brought the two of them to Toledo, chasing after the murderer. Moris had been secretly meeting someone here in Toledo, and Max was almost certain it was Starv. Who else would she know in Spain? If Starv and Moris were in cahoots, then where did that place Max in this sordid story? He had to find out what their game was.

Max went back to Starv's hotel and camped out in the lobby. He bought himself a Monte Cristo cigar, a favorite from his youth. He had also brought with him a Stephen Fry novel he had picked up in the Heathrow airport. He thought, I'll wait here as long as it takes, but I *will* find out once and for all if Starv is staying here. So he sat reading his novel and smoking his cigar, peeking over the top of the pages whenever someone came through the lobby, and tried to make the people fit the description he had been given. After four hours of this, it suddenly occurred to Max that Moris, quite possibly, might have given him a misleading description. Irritated at the time wasted, he collected his book and started back to his hotel.

The darkness had descended quickly on Toledo, and with it the temperature. The air was brutal and gave a sharp sting as it went into one's lungs. The grey lumpy cobblestones were getting a little damp from the night air. Just as Max reached his hotel, light sprinkles of rain began to fall.

Feeling very dejected, Max let himself into his room, turned on the TV, and opened his window. His walk had made his temperature rise. To him it was a nice evening, for he occasionally enjoyed the cold, and a pleasantly chilled breeze came in through the window, bringing with it the sound of voices. Max quickly realized that the voices were coming from the room above and snapped off the television. He sat in the window frame and leaned out a little to pick up as much of the conversation as he could. Faint drops moistened his forehead as he looked up.

One voice was definitely Moris's. The other voice was a woman's, too. He could only make out pieces of the conversation. They might be pacing back and forth in front of the window, and their voices carried as they walked past it.

"So, your new hotel…" Moris moved out of earshot and then back again. "…He didn't see you?"

"No, he never saw me. Of course, it wouldn't make any difference if he…" the other voice said, drifting away.

"He might recognize you," Moris answered. "You've done some bad movies in the past. You should take the bull by the horns and…"

"That's not true, I've been doing my share…"

"Then," Moris replied, "you need…" She faded away. "…Just take care of him…whatever it takes, and get that suitcase."

Max leaned out over open space as much as safety would allow, trying to catch a glimpse of the woman Moris was talking to. All he could see was shadows flitting across the window frame. The voices trailed off, and Max decided that they must have moved away from the window.

He pulled himself up to a crouching position and tried to stand on the windowsill. With fingers pressed between bricks, he attempted to pull himself closer to the room above him, but lost his nerve. Not only was he high off the ground but the sill and the bricks were becoming slippery from the light rain. Shakily, he let himself back down into his room.

Well, Max thought, I was wrong about Moris's secret friend being Antoine Starv. It's a woman, and whoever she is, Moris feels she's not being proactive about getting the case from Starv. This woman changed hotels so Max couldn't get close to her. And apparently she was once a film star of dubious note. The question was: if he and Moris were supposed to be on the same team, why was she keeping this mysterious contact a secret?

Quietly Max opened his door and tiptoed out into the hall. The coast was clear, so Max sneaked up the steps to Moris's room. Outside he pressed his ear to the door and heard the soft murmur of female voices. Maybe five minutes passed before Max could tell that the conversation was winding down. He quickly made his way down the hall and stepped into a dark corner behind a maid's cart.

A square of light spilled onto the carpet as the door swung open. A reasonably tall, slender woman with broad shoulders walked out at a good clip and went into the cage elevator.

Max crept out from his nook and proceeded down the steps with caution. As he reached the bottom, he hesitated and watched the athletic-looking woman leave the elevator.

He could see now that she was attractive, about forty, with highlighted dirty blonde hair. He followed her slight, subtle figure out onto the street. She wore a tight-fitting, brightly colored dress, which made it easy to track her. The woman walked with obvious purpose and weaved in and out of the crowded streets, eventually going into a bar.

Lo and behold, sitting at a little wood table by himself, was a pasty-faced man with white hair. Antoine Starv, his own self.

The woman poured herself into the chair across from him, and Max went to the far end of the bar and tried to blend in. He was so far away that he didn't have any hope of hearing any of the conversation. Body language did tell him a lot, though. He could tell they were not a couple. It looked like a business relationship.

Max ordered a whiskey and watched the show. At one point the woman appeared irritated and Max thought she would storm out of the bar, but she stayed seated. The man always stayed calm and reserved throughout the conversation.

Eventually they got up and worked their way to the door. Out on the street Max ran into a problem. The couple parted company and Max needed to decide which to follow. He picked Antoine, who seemed the obvious choice, since he allegedly had the suitcase.

The woman went down a side street and Max followed his prey down the main street. They walked clear to the other side of the little town, and for a moment Max thought they were going to leave Toledo. Then the man stopped at a nice little hotel.

Starv approached the reception desk and asked the clerk something. Max hung around outside and lit one of the Monte Cristos he had bought. In a moment the hotel manager came out and spoke with Starv for a minute before he disappeared back into his office.

Max was picking a piece of tobacco off his tongue when he almost choked; the hotel manager came back out with an old leather suitcase with double snaps.

Starv collected his treasure and turned to the elevator. Max decided it was about time for a gamble and raced into the lobby to catch the elevator. He wasn't sure if Starv knew who he was or what he looked like, but Max felt that he needed to start taking some chances if he wanted results. Starv slid the cage door closed on the two of them and then looked down at his suitcase. He didn't take any notice of Max. When the elevator stopped, he got off and went directly to his room. Max continued on by as if he were staying at the end of the hall.

Terrific, Max thought, now I'm getting somewhere. That old Sam Spade feeling was coming back to him.

Max ran, giddy as a schoolgirl, down the steps to the street and paced out in front of the hotel, trying to figure out what to do.

He opted for a whiskey and a chair on the street at the bar across from the hotel and made himself comfortable for an evening of surveillance.

6

Max woke up to the sounds of maids talking in the hallway outside his room. God, his head hurt. He must have crossed his alcohol limit at some point during his stakeout. Max pushed himself up out of bed and shuffled into the bathroom. He turned on the shower, picked his shaving kit up off the toilet, and rummaged around in it looking for aspirin. He knocked three back and stepped into the warm shower, which was a hose contraption strung up in a porcelain tub built for toddlers. Letting the water saturate his hair, he tried to come up with a strategy for his day.

By the time he was dressed he had his mind made up. He would leave Moris out of the action, she was too deceptive anyway, and he'd go over to Antoine's hotel. Hopefully Starv would be out, and then Max could break in and take the suitcase. It would be more difficult if he were still in the room, but Max had given himself a pep talk, and he was so convincing that he felt he could take it away from Starv by force. Why couldn't he be a tough guy? He had taught himself how to be a stalker, so he could most certainly teach himself to be a thug. It would be an easy first attempt at thuggery. Starv would be totally unsuspecting.

By the time Max had made it across town to the hotel, he had begun having second thoughts, and by the time he came out of the elevator his legs were shaking. As he approached the door to Starv's room, he realized that he couldn't go through with it. Maybe he should just go back and tell Moris that he found Starv. She would know what to do. She could just seduce the suitcase away from him.

No, he thought, I've got to at least see if he's in the room. If he isn't, all the worrying was for nothing, because breaking into a room doesn't require quite as much courage as socking someone in the nose.

Max walked silently down the hall to the room and knocked. He knocked again, a little louder.

"Mr. Starv?"

No answer. Max jiggled the doorknob. It was locked, but the knob was very old and loose. He cranked the knob all the way to the left, away from the jamb, and pushed his weight against the door. The old wood made a loud cracking sound in protest, but wouldn't give. Max tried another approach. He pushed down on the loose knob, making it support all of his weight. After a few seconds it snapped off with a startling pop. Max put the knob in his pocket and looked into the vacant hole in the door. Poking his finger in the hole, the doorknob on the other side dropped to the floor with a loud crack. He saw the locking mechanism and put his finger through it and slid the bolt out. Pushing the door open, he carefully entered the room, throwing a backward glance to make sure a stray housekeeper didn't see him.

Crossing over to the closet, he looked behind the curtain that was stretched across the opening in lieu of a door.

No suitcase.

Only a little disappointed, he dropped to the floor and looked under the bed. Now he was very disappointed. The bastard must have taken the suitcase with him. The only place he hadn't looked was the bathroom. Max stood up, brushed his knees off, and moved toward the bathroom door with no hope left in him.

Max jumped as if shocked by a wet lamp plug.

There on the floor was a pencil-thin creek of shiny red liquid. It grew from a tributary river that fed from a crimson ocean that had leaked from underneath Antoine Starv's prone corpse. He was face down on the bathroom tile with his limbs splayed out. Max wondered if it was a knife or a gunshot that had done him in, but wasn't curious enough to roll him over.

Max pulled his sleeve down over his hand and used it like a dust rag, quickly wiping down everything that he thought he might have touched. The bedroom door was ajar about an inch, so Max put his eye to it and peeked into the hall. He didn't see any movement, so he casually left the room, closing the knobless door behind him the best he could, and made his way to the stairs.

The lobby had two different families checking in, and all parties concerned were too distracted to notice Max sauntering through. Out on the street he suddenly realized that he still had the doorknob to Starv's room in his pants pocket. A wave of panic swept over him, before rational thought made him understand that the police couldn't trace it to him if he disposed of it. At the exact center of town, halfway between his hotel room and Starv's, he wiped the knob off and threw it in a trashcan.

Max went into a little café and ordered a whiskey and a ham sandwich. What the hell was happening to his life? He couldn't believe it. He felt like Cary Grant in *North by Northwest*, totally helpless and out of control.

Suddenly he remembered putting his finger in the door lock at Starv's room to slide the bolt, and the wave of panic returned to him. God, they'll pick up my fingerprints, he thought. Nausea climbed up his throat from the depths of his stomach. No. No, I poked my finger through and used my finger like a stick, so I never actually pushed my print down on any surface. I should be okay.

He chewed his sandwich slowly. Who *was* responsible? Was it the mysterious B actress or Moris? He had to get away. If he continued to hang around with these people he would end up dead like Starv and Geiz.

Max finished his sandwich and ordered two more whiskeys to brace his nerves.

......

Max ran up the steps two at a time. Once inside his room he quickly packed the few belongings that he had.

He couldn't believe the nerve of Jimmy T. The clerk downstairs had flagged Max down to give him a phone message as he came running into the lobby. The slip of paper read:

"Get your ass in gear, Nancy-boy."

Signed,

Jimmy T. 10:40am

As Max was bent over his bed packing, he suddenly remembered that he never shut the door behind him. He turned around and there, with one arm resting on one side of the door frame and a hip on the other, was Moris Tate.

"What are you doing, Max?"

Max couldn't think of an answer, so he remained silent for a moment.

"Where are you going, Max?"

"Where do you think? I'm getting the hell out of here."

"Why? We have a job to do."

"I'm sick of your games," Max blurted out.

"Games?"

"I'm not going to discuss it. Discussion is a waste of time. You're just going to play coy."

"I don't understand, Max."

"See? Coy! Games! Dead bodies, secret girlfriends—I'm done with all of it." Max grabbed his full bag. He suddenly noticed that at some point Moris had closed the door and was now strategically poised so that he couldn't get to it. He also noticed that the top four buttons on her blouse were open.

"You saw Susan, then?"

"Oh, that's her name, is it?" Max raged at her.

"I thought you were Mister Literature. You don't know your favorite writer's granddaughter?"

It hit Max over the head like a giant marlin. Of course, why didn't he recognize her? The Old Man had a granddaughter that tried modeling and acting and eventually gave up and just contented herself with the modest celebrity she had gained from her own efforts and the Old Man's name.

"Why did you try to keep her presence here a secret from me?" Max asked.

"How could I compete with a beautiful blood relative of your favorite writer?"

"You are *not* trying to tell me that the reason you kept her presence a secret is because you were jealous. That is ludicrous."

Max heard her skirt slide off and hit the floor around her ankles. He tried to find the word "no" in his vocabulary, but seemed to misplace it. He tried to make himself walk out

the door, but roots were growing out of his

feet, digging into the tiled floor. Helpless,

like a condemned man coming to terms with his

fate, Max embraced her, folding over her like

a giant question mark.

7

The sun was starting to set. Through the crack in the curtains, Max could see a blinding sliver of orange light slowly strobe as the breeze pushed the drape open and closed. He looked at Moris on the pillow next to him. Most likely she was pretending to sleep to avoid the uncomfortable feeling of the situation.

Max slid out of bed and retrieved his clothing from the floor. Entering the bathroom, he turned on the shower, and then shut the door. He sat on the toilet and studied the situation and his feelings. Once again he had given into his dark side, once again he had been weak. He remembered there was once a time when he was proud of himself and his sexual exploits. Not anymore.

Max blinked away the thoughts about his morals and moved onto pressing matters. Moris must be the killer. Why else would she seduce him? It had to be a diversion. On the other hand, if she were the killer, why wouldn't she take the suitcase and run? Why hang around? Perhaps Susan was the killer and had the suitcase. If that were true, maybe Moris needed help in recovering it. This latter theory seemed to follow the basic rules of logic, so Max embraced it as fact.

Max, against his better judgment, decided to give it another day to see how things would develop. He thought that he might be getting an ulcer.

Moris looked up as Max came out of the bathroom. He was entirely dressed and his hair was wet and neatly combed. He had caught her in the act of putting on her underwear. She calmly continued to pull them up, acting as casual as possible, but Max remembered their first time together and how her nudity had embarrassed her. Max sat down and watched her finish.

"I found Starv today," Max said in his most offhanded manner.

"Really." Moris tried to sound surprised, but obviously was faking it.

"He had the suitcase."

"Had? Past tense?" Again, Max thought her tone was insincere.

"Yeah, *had*. He lost it. He also lost a lot of blood. Enough to kill him."

"Great," she said as she tucked her shirt into her underwear, clearly disturbed enough to ignore the czars of fashion. "Jimmy T. will not be happy."

"If you didn't kill him then Susan must've."

"I don't think she'd do that." Moris plopped herself onto the bed and slipped her shoes on.

"Why not?" Max felt like antagonizing her. "I'm sure grandpa's money has run out by now, and the acting gigs have dried up. Stumbling onto a lost book by her granddaddy would buy her martinis for a few years. Come to think of it, you never did say why she was here."

"She and Jimmy are combining their efforts." Moris offered quickly. She answered too fast to be lying, although she did buy herself an hour with sex to have the time to come up with the rebuttal.

"You don't think she'd double-cross him?"

"No. I trust her."

"Okay. That's good enough for me." Max tried hard to sound truthful. "Can I meet Susan? I promise not to molest her."

"Sure. I'll call her and set something up for later tonight. I'm going back to my room for a little while." Moris closed the door behind her, leaving Max alone with a room full of suspicion.

......

A couple hours later, Max and Moris sat at a tiny wrought-iron table on the sidewalk. They were chatting about a stray mutt, the strangest mixture of breeds they had ever seen, that was sniffing around their table. The dog had a small body, but it's head was huge, way too big for its torso and shaped like a German Shepard's, except with giant floppy ears. He had very long whiskers that made Max speculate that maybe its mother was a cat.

Moris was giggling at Max's observation, and he was pondering whether it was a courtesy laugh or she genuinely found his joke funny, when Susan walked up. She had a short green dress on and no jewelry. Max wondered if it was because her money was running out.

"Max, this is Susan. Susan, Max."

Max took her hand and stood halfway up to be polite. She took an iron chair and slid it under her bottom with practiced grace.

"So…It's a pleasure to meet you," Max opened with. "I'm a big fan of your grandfather's work."

"Yes, me too."

"How the heck did you get involved with Jimmy T.?" Max leaned all the way back in his chair. He felt his posture made him look relaxed.

Susan glanced at Moris and then commenced to study her napkin. "Oh, at a cocktail party,

I think was the first time. Jimmy was fascinated, like everyone, by my ancestry. After bumping into him a few times in social settings he made me this offer."

Max was inside his own head, reflecting back an hour earlier when Moris had left him alone in his room. He had called Jimmy T. and asked him if he knew that Susan was in Toledo. The old Texan became very agitated, and in fact Max thought he was going to blow a head gasket. Jimmy T. confessed that he was in a race with the author's family for the old manuscript.

"She's not the only one in this foot race," Max added. "A gentleman by the name of Antoine Starv just dropped out. Remember him?" Max chided him sarcastically. "You had Moris working on him, if you recall."

"Oh, he's one o' dem annoying publishers, ain't he…" Jimmy had trailed off in his exaggerated Texan growl.

"Yeah, well, like I said, Jimmy, he dropped out. He won't be publishing any more books. The body count is rising, Jimmy T."

"Stop your whining, Maxine, and git me my book."

Max was considering telling Jimmy where he could stick his book when the Texan resumed his speech.

"If you get me the book, I'll give you a five-hundred-thousand-dollar bonus. If you do not get it, I'll have you killed. Simple as that."

Sitting across the table from Susan and Morris now, Max thought that one or both of them was a hired gun for Jimmy T. He suddenly wished that he had access to a pistol.

"Susan, I'm sorry," Max began, trying to keep it light. "You're probably inundated with questions all the time about your grandfather, but are all of the outlandish stories about him true?"

"I imagine most are. He was a bigger-than-life person. How much of those stories he allowed to be embellished or exaggerated by the media, I'll never know. But just the things I witnessed as a little girl, I'd be inclined to say the stories are true."

"Really," Max marveled. "There are two that I love. One is, he's in a rough quarter in France and a thief tries to rob him—stick him up at gunpoint and take his money. Your granddad says, 'No, I'm taking yours,' and takes the gun away from the guy and bashes his skull with it. He then proceeds to go through the guy's clothes and takes his wallet, leaving the crook unconscious in the street."

The ladies laughed and Max continued telling his tales between their giggles.

"And the other one goes that he was deep-sea fishing with his son. He caught a marlin or something, but then a shark got all tangled in the line while he was trying to bring his fish in. He needs to untangle the shark before he can get to his marlin, you see. Plus, he was worried the shark would break the line and make him lose his fish. The thing lunges and snaps at him. Angered, your granddad hauls off and punches the shark right in the snout!"

"Yeah, yeah," laughed Susan, "I've heard that one as well. I can't vouch for the shark story, as I wasn't there, but I can tell you he kept some French guy's driver's license pinned to the wall in the room he always wrote in. He'd love to tell company that story of how he took the man's wallet.

"One story I *was* present for, was when he got in an argument with a man twice his size. The man was describing all the ways he'd beat up Granddad when, right in the middle of the man's soliloquy, my grandfather draws his knee up into the man's crotch. When the guy folded over in pain, Granddad brings the same knee up again into the man's chin, knocking him out cold on his back like a stuck turtle. When a cop questioned Granddad, he said, 'Hey, I never laid a hand on him.'"

They all laughed heartily.

"But he did have a dark side," Susan added. "By the time I came into the picture his depression was pretty bad. He was not fun to be around. Once he told me that he had never wanted children, and he definitely didn't want grandchildren, especially a girl. He only had one use for women. As companions they were useless to him since they didn't fit into his macho lifestyle." Absentmindedly, her finger skated rinks around the lip of her wine glass.

"I had heard that, Susan. I can't imagine having him as a father. It must have been very hard for your father to be his son. The expectations from that kind of man would be crushing. Who could live up to a man that embodied everyone's concept of manhood?"

Susan nodded. "My father was a mess. He was so insecure from being raised by that testosterone-fueled maniac. Nothing was good enough. Nothing was manly enough. When my father died in that car accident, I was the first to agree with the reporters who speculated it was a suicide. Dad was a very unhappy person."

Max wanted to bring up the fact that her grandfather also committed suicide, but there was no tactful way to approach that subject.

That one single action of the Old Man's affected the lives of so many. It was a trickle-down effect.

They ordered dinner, talked blandly about unimportant things, and sized each other up. They decided they would lay low in Toledo until something developed. Max put all of their meals on Jimmy's credit card, and while they waited for the waiter to bring it back, discussed a sightseeing trip into the country for the next morning.

Outside the restaurant they parted as make-believe friends, closer than Pooh, Tigger, and Piglet. Max walked back to the hotel with Moris.

After making sure she got into her room, Max went back out and bought a world-famous Toledo knife.

......

The next morning found the three
adventurers on the street in front of a small
plaza, admiring Susan's Jaguar sedan, which
looked ridiculously large in the small Spanish
street.

"A rental?" Max asked.

"No," Susan replied. "I keep a studio
apartment in Madrid and have had this car
garaged for years. About eight years ago I was
still getting quite a few modeling jobs, which
required me to live here."

Max could believe that, because at forty-
two she was still very attractive and slim.

Both women wore shorts. Susan sported a
tank top, while Moris wore a bikini top and a
frayed straw hat. Max felt overdressed in
khakis and a white oxford. He hoped the women
didn't notice his sleeve cuffs were starting
to fray as he casually rolled them up his

forearms. The fact that his social class was beneath theirs was painfully obvious to him, but hopefully not to the ladies.

Moris got in the front passenger seat, so Max was stuck in the back. As they drove out of town Max wondered how long the three of them could go without talking about their assignment, the murders, and the two of them obviously being against him. Max listened to the women talk about hairstyles and nail colors for about twenty minutes before he interrupted.

"Susan, do you know Antoine Starv?"

"Personally? No."

"Did you know he was after the suitcase?"

"Y-esss."

"Why was he after the suitcase? Do you know?"

She cleared her throat a little. "He worked for Candor House Publishing."

"*Worked*? He no longer works for them?

Silence.

"Don't try to mess with us, Max," Moris said coolly, "we all know he's dead. Word travels fast in a small town, and all three of us are in the same business. Just because Susan used the past tense doesn't mean you tricked her into an admission of guilt. You are not Columbo."

"Exactly how did the 'word' get back to her?" Max accused.

"I told her, and also, while we're on the subject, if you must know, after you had your temper tantrum and made your display of packing last night, I went to Starv's hotel and saw the police there, just to confirm your story."

"How did you know where he resided?" Max inquired.

"I've been keeping an eye on him," was Moris's response.

"You already knew where he was? I thought we were looking for him. What's this all about?"

"Jimmy T. thinks you're a screw-up since you let the suitcase get away from you in Bath." Moris said it flatly, with no emotion.

"Then why am I still here?"

"Eye candy," Susan interjected, trying to lighten the tension.

They drove in silence for ten minutes, Max stewing in the back seat. However, he *did* like Susan's flirtatious joke.

The countryside rolled by, and Max tried to clear his mind of confusion by distracting himself with the terrain. It reminded him very much of Southern California. There were lots of scattered boulders and clumps of dirty green brush. Occasionally there'd be a long stretch of water-starved yellow field. When they had first set out, the road began curvy as fusilli pasta, but it quickly straightened out. It was starting to bow and sway again and Max was getting motion sickness sitting in the back. Susan pulled off the road without consulting the other two.

"Ready to eat?" she asked. The two women got out and went around to the trunk. Moris came back carrying a large picnic basket.

The car was situated on a slight rise, parked in the shade of a tree. Moris passed out the sandwiches and Susan handed Max a bottle of red wine to open. They enjoyed their meal in silence, and at the end of it Susan suggested a walk.

"You go ahead without me," Max said sulkily. "I'm getting a headache."

Susan put the basket back in the trunk and came back to ask Max if he was sure.

"If I change my mind I'll catch up."

The women left him, crossed the road, and walked up the slight hill, their attractive bare long legs casting long shadows. As soon as they were out of sight, Max bounded over the front seat. He flipped the trunk release and got out. He knew he was fantasizing. He knew there was no way it could be in the trunk, but he had to look and satisfy his curiosity.

Max walked around to the back of the car and slowly pulled the trunk door up the rest of the way. His heart stopped. His breath got caught in his throat.

Max knew his window of opportunity might only be a couple of seconds. The women could be back any moment. Grabbing the old leather suitcase, Max shut the lid quietly, sprinted for the edge of the slope, leaping and sliding down the grade until he reached a clump of

bushes about twenty yards from the road, and
hid the bag under a shrub. Briefly making sure
it was concealed well enough, he ran back to
the Jaguar.

With no sign of Moris and Susan, Max let
himself into the car again, being careful not
to slam the door. He knew how sound traveled
in the country, and it would be to his
advantage if he could lead the girls to
believe that he had never gotten out of the
car. If they thought that he had been out,
even to stretch his legs, they might remember
the suitcase in the trunk and double-check on
it.

The old man's case should be safe under
the bush until nightfall.

Why were the ladies keeping him around?
That question still hadn't been answered to
Max's satisfaction. Possibly one lady, or
both, was trying to not raise Jimmy T.'s

suspicions. If they dumped Max, Jimmy would smell a double-cross coming.

Twenty minutes or so had passed when the women appeared. They were talking as they slowly strolled. Max began to sweat. They were going to check the trunk—he just knew it.

They came up to their respective doors and got in.

"How's your head?" Susan asked.

"Better now." Max smiled.

8

They cruised back to town, Max trying to keep the conversation light, making flippant and flirtatious remarks whenever he could. He wanted to lull the two ladies into a false sense of comfortable friendship. They were all getting along swimmingly.

"Hey, the night's still young, ladies. Let's get some drinks," Max suggested.

They found a little pub, and Max commenced to getting the ladies seriously drunk. Any tool he carried in his toolbox had to be used, to keep the women from checking the car trunk. He knew, being an experienced alcoholic, that he could drink them under the table. Even Susan, who was rumored to have many dependency problems, shouldn't be too much of a problem since her body weight was considerably less than his.

The evening turned into late night, and Max began to see the potential of seducing both lovelies. No, he thought, he must remain focused. Concentrate on the suitcase. But that would be quite an evening, he had to admit. What was the suitcase to him anyway? He wasn't a publisher or a rich Texan. He *was* a womanizer, however.

Actually, if he thought about it, he could have it both ways. After he finished his night of debauchery with the two women, he could sneak out to the countryside and get the suitcase.

The three left the bar, staggering, with Max between the two, supporting them as they stumbled along the inky Spanish alleys. Max's anticipation grew into frenzy. He couldn't believe his good fortune—two beautiful women were coming to his room to share his bed. The feeling took his memories back to his prime.

In Max's teen years, shortly after he received his driver's license, he had a date with a young classmate. He drove to her neighborhood to fetch her on an attractive tree-lined street. After some difficulty, he found the house and trotted up the steep steps to be greeted by the girl's parents, who were surprised that he was so early. They claimed they were excited to meet him as their daughter had told them so much already. She was still getting ready for her big night out, so the girl's mother offered him a glass of iced tea. For the next twenty-five minutes or so, Max swapped stories with the parents in their comfortable living room and seemed to hit it off nicely. Hearing footsteps in the hall, Max turned to greet his date, only to find she was a teenage girl he had never seen before in his life. The odd house numbers ran on the left side of the street, and he had gone into a house on the right side. Mortified, he made his apologies and excused himself. As he ran down the steps, a car pulled up, carrying the intended boyfriend.

Max crossed the street to the right house and continued his evening with the correct date. Driving home afterward, Max had an idea.

The next day he returned to visit the girl with the nice parents. He secretly dated both young women on alternating nights for two months before he was caught. His tandem street romance ended in an ugly confrontation between the two in a shopping mall. And that was the beginning of Max's wicked ways.

Presently, Moris and Susan were in a fit of drunken giggles as they came out of the hotel elevator and made their way to Max's room. Max found that he couldn't get his key into the lock because he would need to release the girls and then they would fall down. He made several tries to complete his task quickly, but as soon as he let go they'd begin sliding down the wall. After many attempts and much laughter, Max figured out a way to do it. He put one woman on each side of the doorknob, with their backs to the wall. He pinned Susan to the wall by placing his left leg between her legs and pushing his hip into her pelvis. He then pinned Moris against the wall by placing his right hand on her breastbone. This left him with a free hand that he could use to unlock the door with. Of course, his risqué manner of holding them up made the two ladies laugh even harder.

As soon as they entered the room, Susan threw herself on the bed, but Moris made a mad dive for the bathroom, from which retching sounds were soon audible. Uh-oh, Max thought, this could add a wrinkle to my plan.

By the time Moris resurfaced, Susan was sound asleep on Max's bed.

"Do you mind if I lie down for a moment?"

"Sure, go right ahead," Max said.

She did and, within minutes, Max heard the sound of two women breathing heavily in a deep-booze coma.

Max sat in his spindly little chair, looking at them, very disappointed.

"Well, back to my original plan," he said out loud. He took Moris's rental car keys and quietly left the room.

9

Max had trouble finding the spot where they had stopped for the picnic. Night changed everything. He began to doubt that he was even on the correct road. Finally, after passing the tree five times, he found the location. He climbed out of the low car and walked to the dirt shoulder of the road. He could just make out the shape of the shrubbery. Sliding down the grade, he had a thought: suppose some farmer's kid found the hidden suitcase? In the event that that had happened, Max decided he would suck on the business end of a shotgun. Hopefully that would put an end to all of his problems.

There it was! The handle of the case was poking out from under some leaves. He grabbed it and sprinted for the car. Plunging into the seat, he engaged the car and spun the machine around in a cloud of dust.

Max steered the auto deliberately, trying to remain in control of his emotions, though his sweaty palms belied his calm performance. He drove through town, avoiding his hotel, and went to the farthest corner of the little village to find a new hotel. It was at that moment he recalled that in Europe you need your passport to check into a hotel. He turned around and drove all the way back to his room.

Max lingered outside the lobby till he saw the young man at the desk get a little swamped. He was trying to simultaneously check in a couple and deal with a drunken patron. Trying to time it perfectly, Max walked in and abruptly interrupted, asking if he could see his passport for a second so he could jot the number down. The reception clerk obliged;

while he moved on to help the couple checking in, Max pocketed his passport and snuck out.

Back on the far side of town, he took a cheap hostel room on the fourth floor of an archaic building. The old lady, who probably owned it, came out from the back, wiping sleep from her eyes. He signed in and paid with his own cash; it would be best not to leave a plastic trail of credit card crumbs for Hansel and Gretel to follow.

He let himself into the small inhospitable room and sat down on the end of the metal-framed bed, placing the bag on his knees.

The suitcase was full. Max looked at it with some trepidation. Two lackeys from two different publishing houses had turned up dead from being in possession of the antique, now it was in his lap. What to do?

He thought about everything that had led
him to this moment: the insane Texan, the two
murders, and the two beautiful crazy women.

Max rubbed the worn leather. So much
sweat and violence over a book. Granted, it's
a book by the greatest writer America had ever
known, but still, it was just a novel.

He moistened his dry lips and undid the
first snap, then the second. He folded back
the flap and looked in at a yellowed, dog-
eared ream of paper about as thick as a
medium-sized city's phone book.

Max pulled the manuscript out of the only
home it had known for ninety years. He
smoothed out the front page with his damp
hands and looked at it for a full minute.

Max decided to read only the first
paragraph, just to satisfy some curiosity. He
soon found he was devouring it, page after
page. He couldn't put it down. The old

feelings of his youth returned to him, the same feelings he felt when he first became obsessed with the Old Man's stories. A hypnotic effect grabbed him with each word he read, pulling at him like a drug craving. Max read through the night until he had finished it, exhausted and spent. It was worth sacrificing his little orgy with Moris and Susan.

He put the manuscript back in its home, slid the case under the bed, and took a quick cold shower to revive himself. He toweled off quickly, dressed, and checked on the suitcase to make sure it was still in its hiding place. I am really getting paranoid, Max thought. He thought for a moment, and then grabbed the suitcase.

As he locked up the room and left, he remembered an old Boris Karloff movie he had watched shortly before he left the United

States. Karloff played a Chinese detective named Mr. Wong, and in the film all of the characters always seemed to be creeping in and out of rooms, hiding behind furniture, and closing doors quietly. Somehow Max had ended up in the story with all of those mysterious characters. He just wanted old Boris to show up in his thick Mr. Wong glasses and tie up all of the loose ends.

Down at the front desk the old lady who had helped him check in had been replaced by an old man, maybe ten years younger than her. Max heaved the battered traveling case up onto the counter.

"Good morning. Do you think you can store this in back for me for safe keeping?"

The man gave Max a steely stare, as if to learn his nature and see if his character was noble. He removed the cigarette from his mouth and blew out smoke with the grace of one who has been smoking longer than he has not.

"Sí."

The old man took the case and went through a narrow doorway behind him. In the small back room Max could see a very thin but attractive woman, about thirty, in a business suit with long brown hair and olive skin. She looked up briefly but then returned to her paperwork.

Hopefully the manuscript would be safe in this family's hands.

......

Max found the two ladies sprawled out on his bed, deep in sleep. Carefully he pulled out Moris's room key from her little purse and let himself out as quietly as he had entered. He trotted up the steps to her room and took it over as his own. When Susan and Moris woke up they would wonder were Max was. Eventually they would make their way up to Moris's room and find Max. He would then explain that since they had passed out on his bed, he spent the evening in Moris's bed. Hopefully, no suspicion would be aroused and they would assume he stayed in all evening.

Max tossed and turned, too excited by his adrenalin rush, and his mind too hyper with thought. After an hour he had just started to drift off when he heard the door creak open. Three women were peaking in at him: Moris, Susan, and a maid with a passkey.

"Well, who's been sleeping in my bed?" Moris said grumpily.

"You two were invading my personal space," Max responded.

"I can think of two spaces you wanted to invade last night," Susan chimed in.

"Yeah, well, I didn't, did I?" Max said, yawning. "I was a perfect gentleman."

"Yes, as far as we can remember," Moris added, clearly the most hung over of the three. "Why don't you clear out and let us get cleaned up? We'll meet you downstairs for coffee."

Max wanted to go to his own room and sleep, but couldn't let on that he had been out all night, so he reluctantly agreed.

He stumbled down the stairs and went into his own room, took a second shower to wake up, shaved, and put on a clean polo shirt. Within twenty minutes he was in the lobby making goo-goo eyes at the front office manager. Max marveled at his own constitution. No matter how tired or sick he ever got, he always was on the trail of a potential bedmate. He was a true caveman.

The girls came out of the elevator, entirely overdressed for the weather, or so Max thought, obviously sending him a message that they would not be getting into bed with him. How scantily clad they had dressed on the previous day, Max mused.

They found a café and ordered café con leche and churros.

"So what's the plan? We're just spinning our wheels here. I want to go back home." Max thought that the quicker he made his exit, the better.

Susan spoke first. "I have to go to London for a book signing, but you two should stay on a little longer."

"You write?" Max sounded interested.

"A gardening book."

"Oh."

"Yes," Moris interjected, "we'll tough it out a few more days. Try to get a lead on where the case went after Starv was killed. We can play Columbo." And with that remark she shot Max a sarcastic look.

"I'd really rather go home." Max tried not to sound like he was whining.

"You can hold out a few more days. After all, you don't want to get on Jimmy's bad side." Moris almost sounded menacing.

"Right."

Susan looked at Max over her coffee, trying to read him. "You can try to find out if Starv had any visitors. Maybe he was seen with people at cafes or pubs." She paused. "*Someone* took the suitcase from him." She added.

"You're going to fly out today?" Max inquired.

"Yes, if I can."

"Okay, then, Moris, maybe we should split up again and see what kind of trouble we can get into."

"Sounds good."

10

Although the sky was a fickle blue like Brooke Shields's eyes, the temperature was quite cold. Max rounded the corner of the hostel at a quick gait and gave one last look over his shoulder to make certain he was not being followed. He trotted up the short flight of steps into the lobby and ran into three police officers, apparently guarding the lobby entrance. Even though it was daytime, all of the lights were turned up to their brightest level, and what looked like a photographer's lamp had been brought in on a tripod to illuminate the reception desk. Men in civilian clothes were measuring distances, dusting objects, and questioning a few people in a stern, professional fashion.

One police officer motioned for Max to approach and began speaking rapidly in Spanish.

"I don't understand. I don't speak Spanish," Max explained.

The officer switched to a decent school-taught English. "What do you need here?"

"I have a room. I just need to collect a bag they are holding for me and then I'll go."

"It is not in your room?"

"No, the manager, or I assume he is the manager, is holding it for me."

"I see," said the policeman, with a quick glance over his shoulder. "When did you drop it off?" He glanced behind him again, at someone advancing in plainclothes.

"Early in the morning. I'm not sure of the time. Maybe eight or so?"

The plainclothes man looked Max over and Max returned the favor, noting the man was short, balding, and thin, but with the makings of what would one day be a paunch by the time he reached his later years. His suit was beige, his sparse hair was beige, his skin was beige, but the pouches under his eyes were a deep purple. When he opened his mouth to speak, Max could see that his gums were colorless, while his large teeth were nicotine stained.

"I am the detective here on this case," he said in heavily accented English. "You say eight o'clock. Can you try and be better exact?"

"I don't think so," Max said. "I really didn't notice the time. What case? What happened?"

The little man cleared his throat. "You may be the last person to see Mr. Camara alive."

"Camara?"

"The manager, or maybe I should say assistant manager, for his wife is the owner of this hostel."

"He died?"

"He was shot."

This is just what Max did not need—to get mixed up in a murder case when he was trying to get out of the country. "Look, Detective…"

"Veloso."

"Detective Veloso, I am a tourist. I just need my bag and then I need to go back to America."

"The reception is holding your passport?"

"Yes."

"What is your name?" Max told him. "I will get it." The little man started to turn but first added. "Mr. Camara was shot just after eight a.m. The time you were at the reception." He walked over and summoned someone from the back office. The pretty

brunette in the business suit came out and
Veloso spoke to her in Spanish, and then she
retreated back to the office.

"That woman!" Max ran over to the
detective. "She must've been one of the last
people to see the manager alive. She saw me
and can tell you that I left."

The woman returned with a passport in her
hand and handed it to the skinny detective. He
spoke to her in his own tongue and Max assumed
he was asking if she had ever seen him before.
She looked at him with sad, unresponsive eyes
and said no.

"What? Yes. You saw me. Remember? You
were in the back and glanced out and saw me."

"I'm sorry," the woman said in perfect
English. "I've never seen you before."

"But you have. I was talking to the
manager—"

"He is not the manager—was not, I mean," she looked scornful. "My mother is. He thought he was, but he was merely her husband."

"Well, I gave your father my—"

"My stepfather. Fernando was my mother's second husband."

"Okay, stepfather, then." Max was getting frustrated. "I gave him a suitcase to hold. An old brown leather one…more like a briefcase."

The woman licked her lips. "I remember Fernando bringing back the luggage. Oh, wait. I *did* see you."

"How do you suddenly remember him?" The detective asked skeptically.

"It was only a second that I looked up."

"Yes, if even that." Max was feeling relieved.

"He left the bag and went away."

"And then what happened?" Detective Veloso asked.

"The rest you know. I went to the fourth-floor storage closet for some supplies. When I was coming back I heard a shot from the landing where I was and found Fernando dead at his desk."

"I hate to be a nuisance," Max interjected, "but since I am cleared, can I get my bag and go?"

The detective paused as he reached for a cigarette. "You can have the luggage as long as it is not evidence. I will need to look at it."

"Terrific. Thanks."

The young woman turned and went back into the office to get Max's suitcase. He watched her and noticed that the body had been removed, for the desk was devoid of corpses.

The pretty woman returned looking even more serious than she had before. "It's not here. It is gone."

11

The police told Max not to leave town and to remain available in case they got in touch with him. He didn't know if he should mention he was occupying two hotels, so he opted not to, thinking it would raise suspicions even more.

It turned out that the manuscript was not the only item stolen. Money from the cash drawer and a small gold statue from the manager's desk had both been taken, and papers had been rifled through.

Nausea pooled in Max's stomach like yesterday's sushi. He could not believe how stupid he had been. He had had the manuscript in his hands. He had even read it. Easy street was just around the corner. If only he had hidden the suitcase better. The theft of the knickknacks and cash had obviously been a diversion to throw the police off the murderer's trail. He or she was trying to make it look like your run-of-the-mill hotel holdup that went wrong. The game was getting more and more deadly and Max was all out of options. It just frustrated him so badly because he was so close to finishing his assignment. It was the first time in years that he had actually felt proud of himself. He had finally accomplished something. And now, since he was some kind of suspect, he couldn't even go home.

Enough time had passed, Max thought, for him to sneak out of his room and return to his other domicile. He'd have to face Moris and Susan and maybe come up with an alibi for them as to where he was. By now Susan had probably noticed the suitcase was no longer in her trunk. The two vixens might have been combing the streets and alleys looking to spill his blood. He left his room and tried to look casual as he crept down the stairs.

......

"Hola." It was the beautiful stepdaughter from the hostel. Max had deliberately tried to catch her eye when he saw her standing in the coffee shop's doorway.

"Well, hello. Sorry, I never introduced myself. I'm Max."

"Yes, I know. My name is Patricia."

"Listen, Patricia, I am sorry for your loss."

"Don't be," she said defiantly. "He was a pig."

"Oh," Max said uncomfortably, and a silence followed that he didn't know how to fill. "Umm…"

"It's okay. There is nothing to say and nothing that can be done. I think he was cheating on Momma, and I have reason to suspect he was blackmailing guests."

"Really?" Max said with interest. Maybe, he thought, it's possible the young woman might have information that would help him find the suitcase. He certainly had nothing to lose and no idea what to do next.

"Would you like to sit down, Patricia, and have a coffee with me?"

She nodded her head and the two went back into the small café and selected one of the two little tables. Max motioned for a coffee to the attendant as he pulled Patricia's chair out for her.

"Thank you."

"Sure. So, step-dad was a bad man. I'm sorry to hear that. It must've made life unpleasant."

"My mother married him after I was an adult, so it wasn't too bad. It wasn't like I had him in my life while I was growing up. Hopefully Momma can finally find happiness now that he is gone."

Max attempted to steer the conversation. "You said he was blackmailing guests?"

"Yes, I walked in on a regular of ours—he stays a lot—giving my stepfather a large sum of cash. Later, when I checked the drawer, there was no money in it. Also, no large payment was on the books for that day. I didn't think too much of it, but weeks later I found a list on the computer of some repeat guests. Next to their names was a code of some sort."

"How many names?" Max interrupted.

"Oh, a short list. Maybe four or five. One of the men Momma and I suspected of having an affair. He'd always check in by himself and later sneak in a woman. It's not the 1950s anymore. You don't need to sneak women into your room, you know? I started thinking that maybe the list was a list of people having affairs."

"You think one of these men, or women, killed your stepfather because he was blackmailing them?"

"Up until now I had thought it was merely a robbery. I guess that is what they intended it to look like by taking money and some items."

"So you haven't told your blackmail theory to the police yet?"

"No. I just thought he was killed in a stick-'em-up."

"Stick-up," Max corrected with a smile. "Do you think you could show me the list? I really need to get my bag back."

"It is no longer on the computer. The next day I looked for it and it had been deleted, and was not in the computer's garbage basket, either."

Max didn't correct her use of English this time, but did find her choice of the wrong words endearing. He also liked how she cupped her coffee with two hands when she drank. Ah, another woman to distract him from the job at hand.

The two went back to the hostel and Patricia invited him into the back office.

"Do you think he printed up a hard copy?" Max asked.

"It is possible."

Max looked around, taking in the cluttered office—the tall narrow bookshelf, the broken nightstand from a bedroom, a wooden filing cabinet, and a desk with battered chair. His eyes came to rest on Patricia's slender form.

"Do you always dress like that when you work?"

"In a jacket? Yes, why?"

"Did your stepfather?"

"No. He wore a musty old sweater. Always the same one."

"He was wearing it when you found his body?"

"No, actually. He was *not* wearing it and had his shirt sleeves rolled up."

Max looked at the chair and it was not thrown over the back of it. He walked to the open door leading to the front desk and closed it. Hanging on the back of the door was a nubby old grey sweater. Max looked for an interior pocket and, finding one, withdrew a sheet of folded paper.

"The list?" Patricia asked.

"The list."

"I should call the police."

"Not yet, okay? I want to see if I can get a lead on my suitcase."

"What is in it that is so important?" She was standing so close to him Max could feel her warmth.

"Astronaut plans." It was the first thing that popped into his head, and as soon as he said it he realized it sounded ridiculous, but he had to commit to the story now that he started it.

"What?"

"It is top secret and I really can't talk about it, but they are designs for a revolutionary new space suit."

"Really? Why are you hiding it from Spain…"

"It's the Portuguese, really. We don't want them to get it."

"But they don't even have a space program."

"I can't talk about it, Patricia. Really, the less you know the better," he said firmly.

She looked bewildered but seemed to buy his ridiculous story and comical attempt at acting.

"The top name is crossed off the list," Max observed.

"That guest died of a heart attack a week ago," Patricia explained. That left three suspects.

"Can you pull the addresses for these names? I want to visit them."

......

The home was what an American might call a brownstone. It was a narrow three-story unit that looked to have been built in the midcentury. Each story had lush flower boxes hanging off the windows. The top floor was shuttered.

"Hola, hola. Do you speak English?"

She didn't, so Max was thankful he had Patricia with him to take over the conversation. They were not invited in and conducted their business on the stoop.

In Spanish, Patricia explained that her stepfather had died mysteriously and they were helping the police look for clues by asking guests who stayed recently if they had noticed anything odd in her stepfather's behavior. Patricia didn't have the chance to broach the delicate subject of the woman's husband staying at the hotel, for she interrupted Patricia's rehearsed speech. Apparently she knew of her husband's affair and had kicked him out a few weeks ago. No, she said, she didn't know, or care, for that matter, where he was living.

That was a temporary setback that deflated Max considerably, but Patricia was now channeling the spirits of great detectives and wanted to move on to the next name on the list.

Hector Dias-Riverte lived across town in a modern stucco home. The plump, aproned wife that answered the door was very suspicious and had obviously been crying. Patricia began with the same speech she gave the last woman, and this time she got a little further. When Patricia reached the part about her husband recently staying at the hotel, the woman began to furtively glance back over her shoulder. Shuffling noises could be heard from the depths of the home. When Patricia bluntly asked if she was aware of her husband's actions, a short middle-aged man, who could be none other than Hector Dias-Riverte, came running out into the entryway, shouting and gesticulating wildly. Patricia apologized profusely and the plump little wife began sobbing and wailing.

As the confusion grew to operatic proportions, Max spied the corner of a leather case in the foyer. Excitedly, he tried to herd the group inside so he could work his way to the suitcase. Once inside he saw it was indeed his bag.

The slight screech of tires and creak of car springs made Max glance outside. A car had just pulled to the curb and inside were two men, including the beige Detective Veloso.

"Police!" Max shouted above the arguing and crying. The middle-aged couple immediately fell to silence, and then the man suddenly turned to run to the back of his home. The woman began crying again, and Max grabbed

Patricia's hand and the leather bag and followed in the direction Hector Dias-Riverte went. At the end of the kitchen a back door was swinging shut after being slammed open to bounce against the house. Outside, Max could see that Hector Dias-Riverte ran to the left down the alley, so Max picked the opposite direction, with Patricia tagging after him.

......

Back at the hostel, Max thanked Patricia and explained that she had done his country a great service.

"You're such a liar, Max," she grinned at him like a tired mother who was too proud of her ornery child to scold him.

12

"I'm afraid I don't understand," Max
said, feeling embarrassed.

The man behind the postal counter was
losing his patience with the stupid American
who didn't have a vocabulary as good as his
three-year-old son. To make the situation even
more frustrating, the foreigner didn't know
how to count.

"I'm sorry," Max apologized, "I can't get
a handle on your money."

The postal employee cussed him out in
Spanish, and then forced open Max's hand and
withdrew the correct amount of currency. He
took the large package from Max and put it on
a shelf behind him.

"Gracias," Max said sheepishly and left.

Well, that was a humiliating experience, he thought, but at least the suitcase was out of his hands and safely on its way to Max's friend's house. Fortunately, he possessed enough common sense not to mail it to himself.

The recipient, Marcus Reimbaum, had been a close friend of Max's for many years. They had been through thick and thin together. Marcus was an ex-hippie that, like many ex-hippies, evolved into an excellent capitalist. As time went by, though, he experienced many failures and setbacks, which had recently set him on a de-evolutionary course back to his hippie ways. He had lost the BMW. In a seedy beach town he took a cheap one-bedroom apartment that was nothing more than a barn-red-colored clapboard shack with running water. Gone was the executive position in a major corporation. The Italian leather loafers were exchanged for flip-flops.

Now Marcus was working as a copyeditor for a small chain of freebie community newspapers, a job which paid just enough for him to keep gas in his aged Vespa. Marcus was a good choice as recipient of the suitcase.

Max got into a rented Citroen and headed for the airport. As he boarded the plane to California, with a layover in New York, he cast a nervous glance over his shoulder. Surely, Susan checked her car trunk before leaving Toledo. Hopefully, she would accuse Moris of double-crossing her before she thought of Max. The two of them fighting would buy him some time. However, maybe they instantly thought of him and were only two steps behind him. He probably used up all of his time during those few hours he was a suspect in the hotel manager's murder. The thought of having two potential assassins close behind made him nervous as hell.

Once on the plane, Max settled into his cramped seat, pressed his head against the crinkly paper napkin the airline provided for his protection against head lice, and closed his eyes. Listening to the engines hum, thoughts bombarded his imagination till Max thought he would scream. Never again would he allow himself to agree to an assignment like this. How was he going to get out of this alive? He ran down the short list of the characters involved in the maddening play that had become his life. Moris, a beautiful liar and maybe a killer. Her partner, Susan, also a probable murderer. And last, but not least, Jimmy T., a crazy millionaire who threatened to whack Max if he failed. The murderer could be any one of them, acting independently or in collaboration with one of the others. The worst-case scenario would be that all three were killers working together with the goal of chopping Max up into little pieces. But if that were true, why would they even need to get Max involved? Maybe they were all just a pack of sadistic beagles that needed a fox to run down. There was too much information for Max to process, so he gave up, ordered a scotch, and tried to sleep.

Sleep wouldn't come. He kept thinking of pretty little Patricia, the sad front desk clerk. She had beautiful eyes…and a beautiful fiancé, too. She proudly displayed him in a frame on her desk. I need to stick to the single women, he mused, and reflected on his numerous dastardly relationships with married women.

The most memorable, perhaps, was Lara. He had this nightly routine worked out with her where he'd pay a visit when her husband left for work, at one a.m. His job was to fill the newspaper vending machines around town and collect the quarters from them. Max derisively referred to him as "The Paperboy."

He would frequently pass The Paperboy on the road just after one in the morning when he was going to tryst with the man's wife. On one fateful morning he passed him, resisted the urge to be a smart-ass and honk, and parked and trotted up the steps to the apartment. Max wasn't sure how many bedrooms the place had. Lara and The Paperboy had two little girls, so, to avoid waking the little ones, Max and she never let their antics go further than the front room.

On that particular night they were just beginning to struggle out of their clothes when a key was heard jingling outside the front door. The sound of the keys crashing to the cement walk immediately followed. The keys were retrieved with a whispered oath, and as they slid into the lock, Lara grabbed Max by

his shirt and bodily swung him around and
shoved him down a nearby hallway. He had no
idea where she was guiding him, but as the
front door opened, she gave a mighty heave and
sent him flying through a doorway into
darkness. As he fell he instinctively tucked
and rolled. In the midst of his tumble he made
out the outline of a bed and aimed toward it
with the intention of doing a neat little roll
right under it. Unfortunately he stopped short
as he slammed into a large wooden box that was
slid under it.

Max became frantic. He could hear that
The Paperboy was now in the apartment, out in
the living room complaining about a lost ring
of vendor's keys. Lara shut the door to the
room he was in but it didn't latch and it
coasted slowly open. He could see Lara and her
husband out in the hall talking. Max reached
up and grabbed the sheet and blanket on the

bed above him and tried to cover himself and make it look as natural as possible.

"Maybe I left them in the kids' room when I went to kiss them goodnight…"

Kids' room?

It was then that Max realized the repetitive sound he had been hearing was breathing, right next to his ear. His newly acclimated eyes saw that a child's head was just above him. He was in the little girls' room, and the box under the bed was a toy chest. It was his moment of clarity. He realized what a horrible human being he was. He deserved to be caught and beaten to a pulp.

Lara had been using her body to run interference and kept herself between The Paperboy and the bedroom door. As he came toward her for a look in the room, she made a bold move and got out of his way.

"No! I'm certain I saw you with them in the kitchen." She ran toward the kitchen and Max soon heard the relieving sound of keys tinkling.

There was the uncomfortable kiss goodbye and then The Paperboy was on his way once again. Lara came into the room and motioned for him to stay where he was. She ran to a window and watched her husband pull away and then she motioned for Max to come into the living room.

He knew the relationship was over. For months afterward he tried to stay away from married women, but he was too much of a scoundrel for that to last very long.

As Max drifted off to sleep in his airline seat, he gave one last thought to Patricia in Spain.

......

The cabby didn't even help Max put his bag in the trunk. Irritated, he slammed the lid down and let himself into the back seat. He told the driver to take him to Coronado Avenue in Imperial Beach. Forty minutes later the Crown Victoria let him out a few blocks from Marcus's beach shack; if the cabby were interrogated later, he wouldn't know the exact address of Max's hideout.

The tiny, sad house sat on a large plot of sand. For privacy, an extremely short, weathered wooden picket fence alternated with a brick wall in guarding the perimeter. It was as if the builder ran out of pickets and finished the job with some spare bricks. The fence would have confused the hell out of the big bad wolf. A small stone border built around the base of the house contained the remains of dead flowers and a living yucca plant.

A few minutes passed uneventfully after Max knocked. He tried again, but still didn't get a response. Now, in the movies, Max fantasized, I'd let myself in and find Marcus dead with a space marked in the dust where the Old Man's suitcase had been sitting. The curtains would stir and out would step Moris in stiletto heels with a pistol aimed at my chest.

The knob resisted Max's tentative twist. Lethargic waves rolled and crashed in the distance, and seagulls screeched their irritating song. A gust of lukewarm air spat sand into Max's eyes. He looked at the weathered window sash to his left and noticed the rusty old window lock. A trip around the side of the tiny house brought him to a window opened about two inches. The screen was barely attached. Max was able to pop it out with his thumb. He slid the sash up and climbed in, pulling his bag in after him.

Motes of dust hung thickly in the dull light that shone through the window. Nothing had changed since the last time he had been to Marcus's house. Paperback books were still stacked up knee-high all around the living room and bedroom like Legos assembled by a demented architect. Three of the four windowsills were used as bookshelves for hardback books. A small dinette table near the couch was buried in books and newspapers. The fireplace, which Max had never known to be functional, was used as a book vault, filled with hardbacks and paperbacks. The faded linoleum tiled floor was mostly covered by frayed throw rugs of every size and color. Dirty dishes filled the enameled sink in the kitchenette, which was technically part of the living room.

After Max's tour of the house, he plopped himself down on the sofa. A cloud of dust swelled up around him. Grabbing a paperback reprint of a Rider Haggard jungle yarn from the end table, Max made himself comfortable for his wait.

Just as Maiwa was telling Allan Quatermain about an evil African tribe, Marcus came home from work.

"Jugg-guga!" Marcus screamed, as he did a comical little dance of fright, jerking and flailing with panic. "What the hell are you doing? Trying to scare me half to death or something? It's not funny. Stop laughing!"

"I'm sorry," Max wheezed. "You should've seen the queer little jig you just did!"

"Stop it."

"You looked like Michael Flatley without the headband!"

"Quit it."

"Marcus Reimbaum *is* 'Lord of the Dance.'"

"Okay, you've had your fun. Why are you in my living room?"

Marcus was a simple man with unkempt orange hair, a few sprouts of stubble on his narrow chin, and silver wire-framed glasses with photosensitive lenses. He wore Puma running sneakers and a faded Billy Joel T-shirt, along with the unconfident smile of a man that cuts his own hair.

Max caught his breath after his laughing jag and explained to him that a package would be coming in a few days in his name. Originally Max wasn't going to tell Marcus the whole story behind the suitcase. He figured the less Marcus knew the better, but at that moment he couldn't resist telling him the wild adventure he had been on. Surely no one would torture Marcus for secrets.

Max unloaded the entire story, bragging a bit about his dalliances with Moris, and glossing over the parts where he was scared witless. The masculine hardwiring that men come installed with did not permit him to paint himself in a cowardly light. He didn't overdo it, though, since Marcus knew he wasn't exactly John Wayne when it came to ruggedness. When he was finished, Marcus blew out a little air and peered at him over the top of his glasses.

"What are you going to do now?"

"I don't really know," Max said slowly. "I have some options. I could take the manuscript to Jimmy, as agreed, but he might kill me to keep me quiet, since he is most likely responsible for all of the killing that's been going on. Or, and this is a big or, I could double-cross him and take it to a publisher myself."

"But then you'll be looking over your shoulder for the rest of your life," Marcus added.

"Right. Either decision doesn't look too attractive. I should never have taken it from Susan."

"Yep. Not your best move."

"I know that! Can you help me with some useful advice, here?"

"Well," Marcus offered, "you could kill the Texan and the two women, that way you could publish the book and not worry about anybody hunting you down."

"I said 'useful advice,' Marcus. That means it must have a modicum of sanity."

"You're in a no-win situation, Max. You could make the transfer for the money in as safe a way as you can, and then disappear. Run to Mexico for a while until you're forgotten by all concerned."

"Yeah, I was thinking along those lines, too. I was just hoping you had some better ideas. I don't think they'll forget about me."

......

Max stayed the night, sleeping on the dusty couch among the paperback novels. In the morning he talked Marcus into letting him stay until the package came, which wasn't difficult since he was going to visit his mother for two days in Valencia. They had some scrambled eggs and toaster tarts and rehashed the previous night's conversation, still without solutions.

After Marcus left for work, Max called Jimmy T. from a pay phone, just to see where he stood with him. Max had never truly known what anger was like till that moment. The

Texan was an ocean of rage crashing down on Max's shore of an eardrum. He bombarded Max with threats and hate. Finally, Max decided to try talking, even though Jimmy had no intention of listening.

"Jimmy, I honestly don't have anything to do with the suitcase disappearing."

"You will die a painful death!"

"Jimmy, listen to me. I just want out."

"My boys will torture you till you beg—"

"Calm down. I really don't know—"

"You thought you could double-cross me? I'm gonna cut off yer—"

Max hung up. He couldn't take anymore. His hands were shaking and his stomach was doing somersaults like a clown at a birthday party. That was the closest to death he had ever come and it was just over the phone. He couldn't imagine what a personal meeting with Jimmy would be like. Slumping down into a

sticky bench outside of the drug store by the
pay phone, Max tried to control his breathing
and sweating.

Reconstructing the events in his head, he
felt that he had drawn the most logical
conclusions. It played out this way: Susan,
finding her car trunk empty, ran to Moris with
the news. They both immediately figured out
that Max was responsible and quickly realized
that he had skipped town. Narrowly missing him
at the airport, they pulled themselves
together and worked out a story to tell Jimmy
T., for most certainly Jimmy was not aware
that they had been in possession of the
suitcase. The girls were planning on double-
crossing the big man—they had to be, or else
they would have told him they had it and the
whole thing would've been over days ago—and
Max put them in a dangerous position by taking
the bag away from them. They had to think

fast. Max was sure that they concocted some story where they were the heroes and Max was the bad guy who absconded with the booty. Judging by the chewing-out Max had received, Jimmy T. obviously had bought into their story and believed that Max had gypped the ladies out of the manuscript as soon as they had stumbled upon it.

Some people fumble their way through life, as if they have no control over it, while others believe that life is governed by the choices they make. At that moment, there on the sticky bench, Max came to believe in a theory combining the two concepts. He felt like he couldn't control anything in his life, but at the same time understood that he had made several unwise decisions, and if he had made better ones, his life may not have been so unbearably complicated. It was time he started thinking before he acted.

Max walked the few short blocks back to Marcus's house, still scared to death, but feeling a little better about his new direction.

That's when the silver BMW with the oxidized hood screeched to a stop next to him.

"Hey! Hey, man!"

Max tucked his chin down and began to walk fast.

"Hey, stop!"

The skinny little man in dungarees and T-shirt slapped his hand on the hood of his car as he came around it to get to Max. Max kept walking as fast as he could.

"Wait! Are you Max? Stop! You won the sweepstakes. And I been lookin' for ya! You got a lot of money comin' to you."

The man was nearly abreast of Max and Max had shifted gears into a run.

"I'll shoot you!" He was fighting with something in his belt and finally withdrew it. It was a snub black pistol and its owner was furtively looking around, making sure there were no witnesses, obviously peeved that Max brought him to the point where he had to pull his gun out in public.

"Whoa-whoa," Max said stopping. "Watch it. You don't want to shoot me. You don't know me. You are looking for someone else."

"No. I've got the right guy. Walk with me." He motioned with the gun for Max to walk ahead of him back to the car. "You were pointed out to me. I know I've got the right guy."

"Pointed out? Where? By who?"

"At the airport. When you landed. We lost you in the traffic at a light. I've been cruising this neighborhood ever since, looking for you."

"You work for Jimmy T.?"

"No. Get in the car."

"What? No." Max said defiantly. "I know the statistics. I get in the car I'm dead. You're never supposed to get in the car because then they can shoot you. But out in the open—"

The little man pounded his little gun into the back of Max's head.

"Get in the car, damn you." He opened the passenger door and shoved the barrel of his pistol behind Max's ear. Holding his pounding head, he slid into the torn leather bucket seat and the door nearly caught his fingers as it slammed shut. Racing around the front, the skinny man awkwardly side-stepped around the nose of the car like a crab on amphetamines till he got to his door. Once inside, he covered Max with the gun using his left hand, and he had to cross it over his right in order to start the car. He steered with his right and rested his gun hand in the crook of his arm, kind of using it to steady his aim. His attention kept ping-ponging back and forth between the road and Max.

"You know," Max said as he rubbed the lump on his skull and tried to focus his eyes. "In the movies the heavy always makes the victim drive so he can aim the gun at him. I've never seen it done this way"

"Shut up." His face was reddening with embarrassment. Max studied him. The man was very young and skinny, with stubbly auburn hair in a military style of cut. He wore a white T-shirt with a slogan written across the front of it that Max couldn't read from his angle. Round knobs of bone stood out on his skinny wrist as he clutched the wheel. Max assumed the wrist that held the gun was the same, but he didn't want to look near the muzzle.

"Where are you taking me? I don't think you know this area very well."

"Shut up."

After watching his erratic driving and the strange streets he chose to turn down, Max realized that the kid thought he was being followed and this was his idea of shaking a tail. In the side mirror Max saw an old Subaru wagon and a late model Jeep. The Jeep picked up speed to follow them through the yellow light and the Subaru turned into a grocery parking lot. What looked like a tail proved not to be, as the Jeep passed them with shirtless teens screaming obscenities at them, voices dissipating in the wind.

"Look, I know you've got to be an employee of Jimmy. T.'s—"

"I said shut up, remember?"

The aging BMW entered the freeway and they drove two exits south and got off again. The area was poor-business- industrial, with Quonset huts and dirt lots and potholed blacktop giving way to gravel driveways. The boy pulled up to a padlocked chain-link fence. He slid the gear shift into park and hopped out to unlock the gate. As soon as Max got his leg over the hump to the gas pedal and his hand on the lever, the boy realized his error and spun around with the gun.

"I'll shoot you," he said in a shaky voice that tried to sound tough. Max quickly withdrew his leg and his hand. The kid tried to unlock the chain with his back partly to the fence. A job that should've taken a few seconds took ten times as long since he tried to keep his eyes on both his task and Max. The gun hand sort of covered Max, aimed in his general direction, and the other hand struggled with getting the key to slide into the padlock. The incompetence was painful for Max to watch. His disbelieving stare made the kid shout "shut up" a couple times through the windshield.

After the gate had been rolled to the side, and the boy had got in, Max muttered, "And I thought I was bad at my job."

The kid's standard reply rebutted his sarcasm.

A tour of the yard included a lot of scrap metal and heavy machines made to crush it and move it around. The ribbing on the Quonset hut was caked with dried dirt that had been splashed up by rain and tractors. Attached in back of the hut was a skinny two-story building, assuredly not built to code. Someone long ago had started to paint it what must have originally been a barn red, but they had given up halfway when they realized they'd need a taller ladder, and now it was a sun-bleached pink.

The boy motioned for Max to get out, and with his gun guided him over to a rickety set of plank stairs. As they approached the steps, the kidnapper couldn't decide whether he should go first or Max should. As soon as he waved Max up, he realized that Max would have the higher ground and could kick the gun out of his hand. He motioned Max back down and took the lead but then saw that his back would be toward his captive, so he turned around and struggled up the steps backward with his gun out. At the top the door proved to be unlocked and apparently empty.

It led to an eleven-by-seventeen room, with a second room hidden behind a curtained doorway. Greasy chipped and curled linoleum covered the floor. Stacks of catalogs covered the linoleum, while a decade's worth of dust covered the catalogs. A desk was to the right, underneath a soaped window. Stacks of receipts and more catalogs covered the desktop. It was some kind of reception office to whatever was in back, as there was a couch and spindly chair for people to wait in.

"Sit there, Max." The kid waved to the wooden chair. As Max complied, the young man took zip ties off the desk and came around behind him.

"Aw, seriously?" Max spat with venom. "This is getting ridiculous! I was sent to pick up a book, not smuggle microfiche in a hollow tooth. For cryin' out loud—"

"I said—"

"Shut up, I know, I know. For Christmas I'm getting you a word-of-the-day calendar to expand your vocabulary."

After fastening each arm to its own armrest, the kid knelt down to fasten Max's right leg to the chair, but Max flung it out, cuffing the boy in the side of the jaw and deflecting his foot to the ear. It wasn't a good connection, it just knocked the kid a little off balance and made his ear sting. He struggled up to his feet, swinging his gun around over his head, and after that Max had no more memories of that morning.

......

A woodpecker with some serious anger issues was pounding away at Max's skull when he woke up. He was more than a little disoriented by the twilight sifting through the soaped window in his plywood prison. The smell of grease, dust, and rotting paper jarred his memory back into the present. His head hurt from the abuse it took, his neck ached from hanging lifeless for who knows how long, and wrists and ankles were stinging from being sliced by the plastic ties.

Wriggling his butt, he tested the sturdiness of the furniture he was bound to. It wobbled a little. Maybe one good spill in it and it would break apart.

"I hear you!" It was the kid's voice in the other room. Presently he came from behind the curtain and sauntered over to the desk, where he lighted on the corner of it.

"So sunshine is awake now." He studied Max with a very mild interest. "Where's it?"

"Tell Jimmy it's in Spain."

"Told you, I don't work for Jimmy. I work for me."

"Then who told you I was looking for the manuscript?"

"Who-wh-who…" The kid stammered with sudden anger. "I am the one asking the questions! You are the one tied in a chair. I want the manuscript or I'm going to torture you. I'm gonna starve you out. I'm gonna go down stairs and get a car battery and hook it up to your—"

"Aw-right, aw-right." Max tried to sound as if he was losing his motor skills and then flopped his head over like he had lost consciousness.

"Oh crap." The kid tapped Max lightly on the face. "Oh shit." He lifted his head up and pulled Max's eyelids open, revealing the whites. "Aw, honey! Honey, you hear me? I think I hit this guy on the head too hard."

"What?" an aggressive female voice screeched from the back room.

"Don't come out, honey. Remember the arrangement." He heard her walking to the curtain and jumped up to meet her.

"Don't come out," he said irritably. Max heard the two walking further back into the apartment. What was going on? Max continued to play possum in case they came out suddenly. He could tell they were bickering, but he couldn't make out what was being said. After about fifteen minutes of discussion, Max heard footsteps and the young man saying he'd be back shortly with food.

"And don't come out here where he can see you. He may recognize you." Then there was the sound of a very sloppy kiss and the boy walked past the chair, squeezed by the desk, and went out the door.

He sat uncomfortably with his neck bent foreword as if he were unconscious for quite a while, fearful that the woman was spying on him from behind the curtain. Eventually the pain wasn't worth the effort. As soon as his head was upright he heard a rustling at the drapes.

"Hello?" he called out, testing the waters. "Why are you and your boyfriend doing this?"

Silence. Then: "How'd you know he was my boyfriend?"

Bingo, Max thought.

"Because of how you two fought. Did you know that ninety-two point four percent of all people seen fighting in shopping malls think they are 'in love'?"

"Really?"

Oh my God. She is as dumb as he is.

"Yes," he added, seeing she'd believe anything. "According to The Salk Institute, anyways, and they should know what they're talking about. From the little bit I heard of your conversation, it doesn't sound like he appreciates you very much. It doesn't sound like love to me."

There was more rustling at the curtains and then they parted and out rolled the undulating Mexican Sea. Waves of hard, compressed fat slithered around her curvaceous frame, quivering with every step. It was Jimmy T.'s secretary. Max had only caught a glimpse of her at the Holiday Inn Tiki Lounge when he first met with Jimmy T., but it was enough to remember her beautiful but heavily made-up face and her sloppy but ridiculously voluptuous figure. She was definitely overweight and very much on the trampy side, but Max still found her attractive in a way.

"You know me?" she tested him, standing pertly in front of him and pulling down her black velvet mini-dress to cover a centimeter more of flesh.

"No," he lied. "Should I?"

"No." She made a big production out of turning around and parading her backside around for him to see. She looked out the soaped-up windows.

The gray matter in Max's head whizzed about as he connected the dots: Jimmy T.'s secretary somehow knew about the Old Man's suitcase and was trying to beat him to the punch. (*Somehow* knew about it? Jimmy T. was most certainly sleeping with her. If Max was attracted to her, then the Texan had to be, too.) She probably had mentioned her assignment of delivering the paperwork to the Tiki Lounge to her pint-sized boyfriend. (He may or may not know about her relationship with her sleazy boss.) Most likely it was the boyfriend's idea to intercept the novel from Max before he could deliver it to Jimmy. The secretary had to stay hidden in the back so Max wouldn't figure out the connection to Jimmy. They'd run away with the manuscript, sell it to a publisher, and live happily ever

after with a big-screen TV and all of the
reality shows they could watch.

She popped her gum, still pretending to
look out the window—*pretending*, Max knew to be
the case, because there was no way she could
see out those panes of glass.

"You know Ronzo is going to torture you,
right?"

"Ronzo?"

"Yeah, Ronzo. My boyfriend."

"Ronzo," Max said incredulously, "is your
boyfriend's name?"

"It's his street name."

"His street name."

"You gonna repeat everything?" she asked.

"Sorry. Look, why don't you untie me?
This is ridiculous, and you seem like an
intelligent lady. You are above all of this, I
can tell. You shouldn't sully your hands with

this kind of business. You shouldn't waste your time on that Gonzo either."

"Ronzo."

"Right. Ronzo. Now I know his name but not yours."

"Silvia."

"Silvia. That's a beautiful name. Wasn't that the name of Miss American back in '97?"

"I don't know."

"Well," Max said, feeling so comfortable in his improvisations now that he knew she'd believe almost anything, "I can honestly say it fits you perfectly. I hear it's the most reoccurring name among the Penthouse Pets and Playboy Bunnies. Did you know that?"

"Really?" She smiled.

"Yes. So how about untying me?"

A sullen-looking pout was all he got for an answer. Silvia walked back and forth in front of him, pulling at the hem of her skin-tight garment some more. Max wondered why some women dressed so provocatively, exposing so much flesh, but then constantly tried to make sure everything that they intended to put on display was covered. They pull their skirts down to cover the most infinitesimal amount of skin. They hold their hands over their already exposed chests when they bend down, and they hold the back of their low-cut pants closed when they bend over. It was the damnedest behavioral oxymoron he could think of. Once Max knew a stripper who even did that. He could remember yelling at her at a party, "You walk around naked for a living! Why are you covering your bosom to bend down?"

"You don't think he loves me?" she said, finally turning from her pacing to face Max. "You said that Salt Institute can tell if someone isn't really in love?"

"Hey, scientists are smarter than me, but I can tell you that from the little bit I overheard between you two, things didn't sound so sweet."

"Yeah."

"I'm no expert on women, but if I had a girl like you I'd sure know how to treat her."

"Yeah? You think I'm pretty?"

"Hell, pretty isn't a strong enough word for you. When God was handing out good looks you went and got back in line for seconds."

"That's the nicest thing anyone's ever said to me," she said while batting her eyelashes and chewing with her mouth open.

"I was thinking that if you put that gum away and came here and untied me, maybe I could show you how beautiful I think you are."

"No," she said stubbornly. "I don't need to untie you for that." She came at him slowly, this time not minding that her velvet dress was sliding up her thighs as she walked. She flared one leg out to the side, making the dress spring up to her waist, straddled him, sitting on his lap, and took the back of his head in her hands.

"Whoa," Max protested. "I'm not into this. Untie me first."

"You'll learn to like it," Silvia said, digging scarlet nails deep into his neck. He opened his mouth to yell in pain but she quickly grabbed onto his lower lip with her teeth and bit hard. A salty taste streamed into Max's mouth and then she began to kiss him deeply. He kissed back instinctively. Talons squirmed under his shirt and he felt the nails go to work again, burrowing deep valleys into his abdomen.

His head flailed back away from her in pain. "Son of a—"

"Don't stop." Her eyes were no longer dull and stupid, but violently alive with a twinkle that was as beautiful as it was scary.

"What the hell is wrong with you? Are you excavating for the last meal I ate? That hurts like hell." He scowled at her. "And take the gum out, please. How'd you like it if I—"

She slapped him hard across the face and then attacked the button on his pants, now worked up into some kind of sexual frenzy. Between the arguing and Max screaming in pain and the woman panting like a dog in heat, neither of them heard the steps on the staircase outside till it was too late.

Silvia was struggling to get her excessive weight off of Max and get to her feet, but her tight dress and meaty physique slowed her down. The door flew open and Max could see Ronzo over Silvia's shoulder, fire in his eyes and thunder in his fist. The pistol was aimed squarely at the two. The expression on the young man's face betrayed that there was no doubt that the gun would be going off any second.

Silvia was halfway up, still partially straddling Max, when his fear peaked into an adrenalin surge and he marshaled his strength into one last lunge. He pushed himself forward with the force of an angry buffalo, throwing Silvia backward into Ronzo, who instinctively fired off two rounds as his lover's sailing body pushed him backward out the doorway and over the railing. Silvia's excessive weight broke the railing and the two fell out of sight.

13

It took a solid twenty minutes for Max to free himself from the chair. He hobble-jumped around the perimeter of the desk until he came to a pair of scissors. Tilting the chair over a bit on two legs, he raised his left hand enough where he could get the scissors into his hand. Clutching the scissors, he pushed himself over backward violently. He had hoped that the fall would break the chair apart, but it seemed to be better made than he had thought. Only one rung had jarred loose at the top, just under the armrest. Fortunately, it was a rung that his left hand was tied to. He worked his bound hand up the wooden dowel, sliding the plastic zip tie along. When he came to the top of it, he pulled hard, using leverage to break the wood the rest of the way free and slip his hand to freedom. Reaching over, he grabbed the scissors from his right hand and cut the remaining straps.

It felt good to have the circulation back in his hands and feet. Max walked over to the doorway of the little office, not sure what to expect down at the bottom. Hesitantly, he walked over the broken banister and peeked over. Lying on the ground below, splayed out spread-eagle on the cement patch, was an ugly mess, eight limbs jutting out in every direction like a deformed starfish. Nothing seemed to move, so Max went down the steps to the ground. He approached cautiously and didn't get within arm's length, in case one of them was faking death and tried to grab him as the serial killers always seem to do at the end of the movies. But neither one of them, Ronzo nor Silvia, would be doing any lunging again. Ronzo, who was crushed under his girl, had his head tilted at an impossible angle, and an explosive red spray covered the pavement beneath it. Silvia probably had two bullets lodged in her back, but Max wasn't going to flip her over to find out. She was obviously dead, for if she were alive her false modesty wouldn't permit her to have her dress pulled up to her rib cage.

Back up in the office, Max wiped down the edge of the desk where he thought his fingerprints might be, and then he picked up the remnants of the chair, broke it into smaller parts, grabbed the zip straps, and threw everything into a burlap sack he had found in the back. If he left no evidence that a third person was there, maybe the police would just think that Silvia and Ronzo killed each other in a lovers' brawl.

He slung his sack of broken chair parts over his shoulder and stopped to take one last look at his would-be kidnappers. Maybe, he thought, he should call the police and try to explain everything. But it all sounded crazy. They wouldn't believe him. And his assignment—what with the stolen novel and all—was kind of shady from the start. He'd be looked at as a criminal, for sure. If Jimmy were backed into a corner he'd claim Max knew everything from the very beginning and was involved in the murders.

It suddenly hit him. His skin was under Silvia's finger nails and his blood was in her mouth. His DNA was everywhere. Should he wash it off? Should he look around for bleach and clean her up? But if the presence of bleach were discovered, then the police would probably start looking for a third person. They'd also be able to tell if the bodies had been moved. On TV they always seemed to be able to tell somehow. Maybe they'd think it was a domestic fight and not bother testing for DNA. Do they test no matter what? He didn't know. He remembered hearing it was an expensive procedure, so maybe they only looked for DNA if there was cause to. Finally, he decided to leave things as they were and turned to walk away.

But the bloody skin under her fingernails was pretty obvious. A coroner would spot that right away. Turning back, he studied the bodies and pulled at his lip. He knew he was wasting too much time here. What's that? He bent over the corpses. All along Ronzo's neck and arms were deep scratch marks, some partly healed and some fairly fresh. Hopefully the police would assume the skin and blood was Ronzo's. Max had no choice, really.

Max turned reluctantly, left the property, closed and locked the gate, using

Kleenex to wipe for prints, and then started

his long walk home.

14

His third day back in the US was mercifully uneventful. He stayed indoors all day long, fearful that if he stepped out he'd be dodging bullets, psycho women, and cops faster than a groom ducking fistfuls of rice.

The news hadn't been carrying any stories of murderous crimes of passion in seedy industrial parks, so Max viewed that as a win, although it did prolong the suspense. He kind of wished it were all out in the open so he would know where he stood with county law enforcement.

On the fourth day the package arrived from Spain, and Max was very happy because he felt he was developing some kind of lung affliction from living in the dust-bowl house. He didn't bother unwrapping the box; he just

sat down with it and tried to think of the
perfect hiding place. Now if I were Captain
Clegg, where would I bury my treasure, he
thought?

15

Max had sat across the street from his own apartment in a borrowed Chevy Nova for eight and a half hours. He had brought a lot of snack foods, beverages, and an empty milk jug to pee in if it came to that, and it had, about six hours into his stakeout. The Nova was borrowed from a woman that still spoke to him. He suspected he was still on good terms with her, because she hadn't been looking for a relationship or even a returned phone call. She led an extremely casual lifestyle, one she described as "like a bird with no cage and awfully big wings," and Max speculated that she was probably one step away from prostitution. She could always be found in one of the local watering holes, and more times than not, when he ran into her, she came home with him. They had a semi-frequent one-night-stand type of relationship for about a year now, and, at the moment, he couldn't recall her name. It was on the tip of his tongue and he knew it started with an R or a T. At least he knew it started with a letter on the far end of the alphabet.

R or T worked odd seasonal jobs, and then, when she was laid off, she would collect unemployment for as long as she could. That was her routine. Also, she depended heavily on the charity of male friends. When Max had first met her, she was working at the race track in Del Mar, mucking stalls, painting rails, and planting sod. Her favorite work outfit was an ancient one-piece bathing suit that was white and so threadbare from age it was entirely see-through. She wore no bra underneath and sported this frail one-piece in conjunction with a pair of sweat pants made for a child. The first time Max set eyes on her, he was seated at an outdoor bar watching people pass on the sidewalk. R or T crossed the street, wearing the white outfit, heading directly toward him; a gawking truck driver smashed right into a Mitsubishi. She later told Max the same thing happened at the race track, but it was a tractor that crashed into a horse. Max told her she was the only woman he knew whose looks could stop a horse dead in its tracks.

He could see his own car across the street with two parking tickets on it. Nothing unusual had happened while he had been watching. And being stagnate had begun to take its toll on him.

Another uneventful hour passed and Max thought that he would pull his lips off if he spent another second in the car. Surely he had been careful enough. No one was watching the apartment, and thugs weren't hidden in alleyways waiting to pounce on him.

Cautiously, he climbed out of the Nova and looked around. A child was playing in the gutter with a headless G.I. Joe doll, one of the old ones from back when G.I. Joe was tall and had real hair, and a little further up the street an obese woman in a paisley muumuu was waiting for a bus.

Max crossed the street to the three-story stucco building and entered through the turquoise security gate that was never locked. Passing the elevator, he entered the stairwell and silently climbed to the third floor. The hall was clear, so he crept to his apartment. Outside, all seemed quiet and ordinary. Max pressed his ear to the door but didn't hear anything. He thought of a movie he once saw were a man carefully put his key into a lock and the door exploded, blowing him to pieces.

Max carefully put his key into the lock. Nothing happened. He thought that maybe in the movie the man had turned the key to trigger the bomb. Swallowing hard, he turned the key in the lock, and jumped a little when the bolt snapped loudly. No, no, now he remembered: the man pushed the door open, which tripped a wire that triggered the detonator. Max opened the door as slowly as was humanly possible.

The apartment smelled very stale from being shut up for so long. It looked as if nothing had changed since he had left for England. There were still a few dirty dishes in the sink. Clothes were still draped on chairs and on the couch. The bed was still a mess, a mixture of sheets and clothing. It didn't look as if anyone had been in to toss the place. If someone had been there, they were pretty neat.

He went into the kitchen and poured himself a whiskey. Sitting down in his lounger, he took a deep drink and commenced to speculate. A new wrinkle had creased his theory. Max thought that Jimmy would have had people search his apartment and stake out his building, but there weren't any signs of that.

However, there was a book on the floor near his feet that was opened and lying face down. He picked it up, trying to remember if he'd dropped it there before he left. *The History of Scotland*. Max hadn't looked through the book in years. Moving slowly to the bookcase, he slid it into the empty space next to a book on Spain. Kind of a coincidence, he thought, since he had just gotten back from Spain. Removing his fingers from the book on Scotland, he pulled out the book on Spain. A few sheets of folded paper fell out. Picking them up, he recognized his own handwriting. A

fragment from a story he had written. He
backed up with it and sat in the chair.

> She did not have the exaggerated
> curves often associated with
> feminine beauty. Nor did she possess
> the waif-like thinness of a runway
> model. Her type of beauty was of the
> unique type that falls in between
> the two, where an economy of line
> exists. It was as if God used just
> enough ingredients to fill out her
> figure, no more and no less—nothing
> wasted, but just the exact amount
> needed to get across that she was
> desirable.
>
> Long brown hair of a robust
> color flowed luxuriously down her
> back, hanging in waves with a mind
> of their own. Her beautiful hair was
> so thick that it actually stood away
> from head and body when you looked
> at her in profile. She would never
> want for hair.
>
> Her skin was a creamy pale color
> that contrasted nicely with her dark
> hair, marking a
> stark extreme between the two
> hues. She had a lovely face,
> tapering down a defined jaw line to
> a small delicate chin, with a
> beautifully pink mouth above. Pale
> grey-blue eyes that were large, but
> not overly so, appeared to shine
> under long lashes. They seemed to
> always have a wet quality and,

combined with their light
color, made the sunlight catch there
and sparkle, making her smile that
much more attractive. Countless
types of smiles crossed her lips:
the nervous and hesitant smile when
she was unsure of herself; the
beautiful planned smile for photo
opportunities; the mischievous elfin
smile when she was enjoying a good
time, sometimes at someone else's
expense; the pleased smile for when
she was proud of what she had said
or accomplished; and the most
beautiful of all of them—the smile
when he made her laugh.

Her face at rest could display the
ice-queen looks perfected by old
noir film starlets from the 1940s,
but could then shift into a frown
that made her look girlishly
cute, and the very next second,
change the previous expressions into
one of warmth and compassion,
showing that the sober face before
didn't accurately reflect what was
truly going through her mind.

Personalities are intricate things,
and to get to know her and find her
true personality was difficult. It
is only after a year or so of
knowing her that one begins to see
the hints of how nice, how fiendish,
how gentle, how wicked, how
innocent, and how clever she can be.
All of these traits were mixed
together into a wonderfully fun bowl

but hidden away in a cupboard of shyness that one must search through to find.

She had a way about her, for right or for wrong, that warmed him to the bone, and he would never forget her, or the feelings she instilled, for as long as he lived. In fact, the man had a dreadful fear. Perhaps it was because he realized happiness is ephemeral, but he feared losing her. He had an irrational feeling that something bad, an accident maybe, or perhaps a sickness, but something or other would steal his chance at happiness, taking her out of his arms—for life can be bitter and cruel.

It had been about Nanna, or, actually, the character had been based on Nanna. He wrote it when they were dating. Those last two sentences betrayed that he knew what was coming, knew that he was going to lose her. After all the years that had passed, he still felt the icy shock of a lost breath whenever he remembered losing her.

"So many wasted words…" he muttered aloud.

Something stirred in the other room. He leaned over the armrest of his chair and could see directly into his bedroom. All of the clothes and rumpled sheets on his bed were moving, being shoved around by their own private earthquake. The sheets flew off, exposing a totally nude woman.

It took Max a moment to realize that it was Susan.

"Hello there." He tried not betraying how startled he was. "I didn't recognize you without your clothes on." He pulled himself up out of the lounger and shambled into the bedroom in what he thought looked like sophisticated ease, as if a nude woman in his bed was a more-than-common occurrence.

"Can I have one of those?" She pointed to his drink.

"Be right back." He relocated to the kitchen. "Please, don't get dressed on my account."

Susan gave a courtesy laugh.

"Whiskey okay?" Max hollered.

"Sure, just cut it with water and ice."

"Sissy."

Max tried to play it cool and act unruffled. She must be onto him and angry as hell about him stealing the manuscript. The good news was she was not packing a gun. He desperately tried to think his way out of his predicament. He came around the side of the bed and handed Susan the drink. She didn't appear to be the least bit embarrassed by her nudity.

"Nice outfit." Max said dryly.

"Oh, this old thing?" She sat up even straighter to accentuate her odds and ends.

She obviously knew that she didn't look her age.

"Yes, it sets off your eyes," Max replied.

Susan pulled Max down onto the bed so that he was sitting next to her.

"All of this attention wouldn't have anything to do with a missing manuscript, would it?" Max asked.

"Now that you mention it, Max…"

Her lips were very close to his face all of a sudden, and he thought he felt a nipple brush against his shoulder.

"Look, I need the manuscript, Max. Without it we're both dead. There is enough money for the both of us. I need your help."

"I don't think Jimmy T. is that forgiving, Susan. I've crossed him. He'll kill me no matter what." Max definitely felt a nipple that time. "You are obviously more forgiving. I tricked you, remember?"

"It hurt, but I guess I wasn't being honest with you either. We can pool our resources and get through this together…as a couple."

"I see."

"My idea is that I take the suitcase to Jimmy, instead of publishing it myself, leaving you out of it so you don't end up dead, and then we take the money to Mexico and live happily ever after."

"I don't know if that would work." Max pretended to be interested in a stray sock he found in the bed. Susan climbed into his lap.

"We'll make it work."

16

Max spit the used toothpaste into the sink and noticed that the stream from the faucet formed a heart-shaped pool of water in the basin. He contemplated the stream's point of contact in the bowl made the dimple at the top of the heart, and the flow of the water as it sloshed around the sink formed the point at the bottom of the heart. He had never noticed the effect before. God, he thought, the relationship he had with these two women was about as far removed from love as anything could be. Why in the world was he seeing hearts in his bathroom sink? Next he'd be mooning over flower shapes in the clouds.

"Whatcha thinking about?" Max could see Susan in the mirror standing unguardedly naked in the doorway behind him. How different from Moris with her sheets and towels and modesty.

"What happened to Moris?" Max asked.

"She stayed behind in Spain to tie up some loose ends."

"What kind of loose ends? Antoine Starv is dead. I ran away with the suitcase. There is nothing left there for her."

"I don't know, Max. She was talking to Jimmy when last I saw her, and he had some work for her to do."

"Which of you two killed him?"

"Starv? She did, of course. You know how cold she can be. I don't have it in me."

Max envisioned the two women playing good cop/bad cop with Starv, like they had been doing to him. Moris: the cold, aloof one that he had to extort into sleeping with him. Susan: the friendly one who seemed to be genuinely interested in him. Two sides of the same evil coin. Starv probably never knew what hit him, what with two beautiful women messing with his mind, playing with his emotions, or hormones, or whatever. Maybe they were tag-teaming Max. Moris failed, so now she passed him off to Susan.

In Max's college days there had been two girls interested in him at the same time. The only difference was that the college girls weren't trying to use him to get anything. One wanted a meaningful relationship with him, and the other just wanted a few meaningless nights with him. Unfortunately Max had chosen wrong and ended up wasting three years of his life in an unhappy relationship. He often wondered what direction his life would have taken had he picked what was behind door number two instead. Life would have been drastically different, Max was certain. Jobs were turned down, career choices altered, and many plans compromised because he was in a relationship that he shouldn't have been in. If instead he had gone with the party girl who just wanted a fling, his young adult life would have been more on track. It was strange to think that the "bad" girl probably would've been the right choice.

But now that Max was at the point in his life where he should be settling down in a relationship, he was bed hopping. He seemed to always have the right attitude at the wrong time in his life. Did he secretly yearn for a meaningful relationship? Or maybe he was letting himself become so deeply involved with these vixens because he was experiencing some kind of bizarre mid-life crisis, repeating his college days, but this time with two murderesses. Did he want to settle down with one of these Lizzie Bordens? Max decided that if he got through this alive, he would need to see a therapist.

No, screw the therapist. He didn't secretly long for a relationship, he decided, suddenly remembering Nanna. He never wanted to go through that again. The one time he *was* truly in love ended in a lot of needless pain.

"Let's go get the suitcase, Max." Susan had perched her nude self on the toilet lid.

"I can't. It's not here yet. It's on a slow boat from Europe." That should buy him some time, he thought.

Susan looked as if her lawn mower had sucked up a groundhog, and now she didn't know what to do with a broken Briggs and Stratton.

"I need to go into work and see if I can get them to hold my job a little longer," Max lied. "Are you staying here till I get back?"

"No," Susan answered. "I need to meet with some people from a makeup company that is using my face."

"Ah, a modeling gig."

"I guess. When a model gets to my age the work they get is for advertising anti-aging creams."

Susan walked over to the side of the bed where her clothing was. She slid into her pants, stuffed her underwear into her pocket, and pulled her t-shirt on.

"Maybe I'll see you tomorrow?" She gave him a quick kiss and made her exit.

Maybe, indeed. Max knew that she would be close by until she got sight of the suitcase. Her big brass ring.

A little makeup bag that did not belong to Max was sitting on the back of his toilet tank. Max had no scruples about going through Susan's personal belongings. All the usual female accessories were in evidence, but there was one curious item: a little green bottle filled with a clear liquid. The remains of a prescription label were still stuck on the bottle. It didn't smell like anything when he sniffed at the contents. Probably poison or knock-out drops, Max mused, meant for him. He slipped it into his pocket so it wouldn't wind up in one of his drinks.

How the hell did she get into his apartment?

......

The police had just come down hard on Bogart for being insensitive about the death of the girl that had spent the evening with him when Max's phone rang. After three rings the machine answered for him and Max heard a familiar twang of voice.

"Boy, ya better answer the phone 'fore I kick your head in."

Ice trickled down Max's spine. He got up off the couch and turned off the TV.

"You had better git out of town before I dice you up like some Chinese vegetables."

Grabbing his bag, which was still mostly packed from his trip, and picking up his keys, he made a dash for the door. Darting out the door, he nearly ran into a silhouetted statue that someone had placed directly over his welcome mat. After recovering from the surprise, Max realized that it was Jimmy T. with a cell phone in his ear and an enormous grin across his face.

"Where's the fire, boy?"

Max took two steps back, actually staggered back, affected by the shock.

"Let's have us a little powwow."

Jimmy came in and shut the door behind him. He walked into the kitchen immediately on the right and began going through the cupboards.

"Where do you keep the scotch? Ah, here it is." He poured himself a glass and took a mouthful. "You should treat yourself better. 'Twouldn't hurt you to spend a little bit more an' git the good stuff. 'Specially with a guest comin' over, and all."

"I don't have the manuscript." Max finally found the strength to speak.

The Texan looked pained. "O'course you do. We ain't going to play that game."

Jimmy came around to Max's side of the breakfast bar and Max switched with him, taking his place in the kitchen.

"Don't make me play rough, Maxie-girl." Jimmy T. nonchalantly pulled a revolver out

from under his sports coat and simultaneously
drained the last bit of scotch from his glass.

Max took a glass from the dish drainer
and made himself a drink. "Look, Jimmy, I'll
tell you the same thing I told your little
assistant: I don't have it. Can I get you a
refill?"

Jimmy slid his empty glass across the
Formica breakfast bar.

"I have a strong suspicion that those two
cuties of yours are playing monkey in the
middle with you, Jimmy."

Suddenly, Max felt a surge of excitement:
he had Susan's prescription on him! Slyly, he
pulled Susan's little green bottle out of his
pants pocket with two fingers. "I don't know
what those women have been telling you, but
the last time I saw that suitcase it was in
the trunk of Susan's Jaguar in Spain." Max
turned his back on Jimmy and poured the

contents of the green bottle into his glass.

He reached for the scotch and added it on top

of the liquid, silently hoping that the bottle

wasn't just migraine medicine.

"Now, boy, do I look like a monkey to

you?"

"Ice?"

"No."

Max passed him the hopefully lethal

cocktail and prayed that it didn't taste

strange.

"Jimmy, I'm being honest with you. Those

two women played me, took turns seducing me,

and tried everything in their power to keep me

off balance. You can't trust killers, and that

is exactly what you are in league with."

"They were doin' a job," Jimmy said after

a quick sip of his drink. "An' they were

following my orders, so I trust them more than

I trust a little piss-ant who can't afford

decent whiskey." He set the glass down roughly, and looked as if he had no intention of finishing it.

"I'm telling you that they intend on keeping the manuscript, publishing it, and splitting the money between them. They are double-crossing you."

Jimmy suddenly looked very angry, grey and blonde eyebrows knotting themselves together, and he pointed the revolver directly at Max's head.

"Why can't you see it, Jimmy?"

"You are going to take me to it. End of conversation." Like a true alcoholic, without thinking, Jimmy picked up his foul-tasting drink and finished it in a single swallow.

"I'm sure you're smart enough not to keep it here, an' I've had the joint tossed, but let's have us a look around anyway. Just to be on the safe side."

He waved the gun at Max, motioning for him to walk ahead of him into the bedroom. Opening the closet, he said, "Pull all of that stuff down." Max did as ordered, taking all of the stacked sweaters off the shelf and bringing down the two cardboard boxes. Jimmy kicked all of it over and moved Max's belongings around with his foot.

Max continued to search through everything that Jimmy told him to. He kept watching the old man's face, looking for some sign that the drug was having some kind of effect. Jimmy had him turn over his mattress and box spring. He took the back off of his toilet tank, pulled off the upholstery under all of his furniture, and took everything out of all of the cabinets. When they came to the bookshelf in the living room, Max spotted his handwritten pages about Nanna. He felt his face warm and hoped Jimmy T. wouldn't read them. He wasn't' sure if he was embarrassed because it exposed his soul or because the writing was so bad.

Jimmy hooked some fingers from his free hand into some book bindings and yanked them to the floor and motioned with the gun for Max to do the same. It was then Jimmy stopped distractedly. He saw the pages, opened them up, and with the other hand used the gun barrel to push his cowboy hat back on his head.

Anger at having his privacy invaded pumped through him. With the gun momentarily off him he had a chance for a lunge. While he debated what to do, the moment passed and the gun swung back in his direction. As the fat man silently read, his lips moved with the words and then curled into a sanctimonious grin. His eyebrows grew tighter together and he let out a whooping laugh.

"That's downright sweet, Maxine! Downright purty, I'd say. You've got quite the sentimental heart. Hey, I tell you what, Maxi-pad, maybe you and I can rent some o' them Julia Roberts movies and have us a good cry together."

Max scowled in shame and dug his nails into his thumbs to keep from hitting the fat man. Jimmy walked past, cuffed Max on the back of the head, and announced it was time to get back to work. They pulled down several shelves of books together and left the living room looking like a post-apocalyptic library. To see all of his wonderful books thrown around with abuse placed a sick feeling right in the base of his stomach. Of all people, Max thought, you'd think a fellow collector would be more respectful of books. But Jimmy was in it for the money; he had no love for words.

"All right!" Jimmy T. had worked himself up into a lather. "Let's get to your car. You are taking me to where you have the manuscript stashed, or I'm putting a butt-load of bullets into your cranium."

"Jimmy, I'm telling you—"

"Move!" Jimmy cuffed Max again in the head with the side of his gun.

They went down the stairs and Jimmy's steps never faltered, his gun hand never wavered. Max decided that it must have been an appetite suppressant that he had slipped into the scotch.

They got into the borrowed Nova, Max behind the wheel, Jimmy T. riding shotgun with a gun.

Becky! The name of the girl with the see-through bathing suit that owned the Nova finally came to him. Why did he think her name started with an R or a T? Ah-ha. Rebecca. So he was sort of right.

"Where are we going?" Max asked.

"Don't play funny, Nancy-boy! Drive."

Max slid the stick into gear and pulled out into the sparse traffic. He took surface streets, avoiding the freeway, and headed downtown. He deliberately tried to pace himself so that he hit red lights. If he wasted enough time, maybe the drug would knock the millionaire out.

"Tell me, Jimmy, why would someone who is as obscenely rich as you are want to publish this book so badly? It's not going to bring you *that* much money. I'm sure you'd make more money on a single oil deal."

"Some of it's the money, but most of it is passion. Just like you, boy. Plus there's a lot of prestige involved. I wouldn't need to play the good-ol'-boy rich redneck part anymore."

Max noticed the twang slipped out of his accent and wondered how much of the Texan's personality was a performance.

"You're losin' your Southern accent, Jimmy T.," Max said, mimicking his drawl.

"Lissen here, sissy-pants, I don't speak Southern. I speak 'ranch.'"

"Wow, there for a second you were almost sensitive, what with opening up about yourself like that, but then you had to ruin it with that sissy-pants comment."

"Shut up." Jimmy audibly slurred the words. "What are we doin' here?"

Max angled the car in toward a curb.

"This is where the bag is," Max said as he put on the parking brake.

"Here? At the train station?"

"Yep."

"Oh, that's rich! Is it in a public locker?"

"Yep."

"That's rich, boy! Not very original, but very ironic, hiding the bag in a place like it was originally lost from a hundred years ago. You've got style. A little too much sugar in your ass, but you've got style just the same." Jimmy yawned and looked as if he were struggling to keep his eyes focused.

"I'll wait here," Max said.

"No you won't. You're comin' with me."

They got out of the car and Jimmy stuck close to Max, his hand in his pocket, close to his gun. Stumbling on the curb, Jimmy fell against Max's shoulder, but Max didn't have the presence of mind to try and escape.

"Don't try anything funny." The Texan poked Max in the ribs with the revolver through his jacket pocket.

I wonder, Max thought, if I should let this idiot know his secretary and her inbred street-hood boyfriend were going to steal the book from him? No, better not to incriminate myself in that fiasco, he figured.

They entered the old lobby through the double doors and made their way to the storage lockers. Max had envisioned the lobby being crowded with hustling and bustling passengers forming a distraction for his escape, but in truth, the lobby was quite empty. Life was not a Hitchcock movie after all, and he was definitely not Cary Grant. And Jimmy T. was no James Mason.

An old janitor, face wrinkled like un-pressed laundry, slowly pushed a cart passed them. A tiny radio hung on the end of his broomstick, stuck between stations. One second it was a Joe Cocker song, the next it was Mariachi music. It made for a bizarre mash-up.

Max wondered which station the man was trying to listen to.

"I'm gonna sit down here while you get the bag," Jimmy said as he slumped down onto a bench. Max noted that the millionaire could barely keep his eyes open.

The lockers were only six yards away, but Max tried to drag it out. He looked over his shoulder at Jimmy when he reached the tiny storage unit, and the Texan had just snapped his head up from a brief doze. Max fished a key out of his pocket and put it in the lock. As he pretended to turn it, he cast his head around again for another glance at Jimmy.

Jimmy T. was out cold. His chin was on his chest and his bottom lip was stuck out like a hound dog's on a back porch.

Max put the key back in his pocket and walked nonchalantly by the old man. He didn't want to draw any attention to himself. The last thing he needed was someone chasing after him yelling, "Mister, you forgot your father."

As he passed him he studied the old face, trying to see if he were dead or merely asleep. It was impossible to tell, so Max proceeded on out the door.

Getting into the car as quickly as possible, Max ignited the engine and pulled away from the curb. Heading out of the downtown district, he decided he would run back to his apartment, get everything of importance out of there, and meet up with Marcus. He was going to need to find a new place. He didn't want to endanger Marcus's life by staying at his home.

17

The little beach house looked vacant. Max had been loitering on the sidewalk for about twenty minutes, making sure no one was there. He let himself in using the spare key Marcus had loaned him. Nothing looked different. All of the clutter and dust were still present. A note on the kitchen counter told Max that Marcus was back in town and at work and would be home by six.

Max turned on the small television set on the milk crate so he would have a little company. Some kind of Japanese cartoon was on. Max fondly remembered the Japanese neighbor that helped him translate his childhood shows, and wondered if she were still alive. The time passed slowly in the tiny house. Max amused himself by doing the dishes in the sink, reading a little in some of the books that were stacked around, and looking through a photo album he came across.

There were a few photos of women that were probably old girlfriends of Marcus's that Max either didn't remember or hadn't been introduced to. There was one picture of a particularly beautiful woman that Max had forgotten about. Maybe six years ago Marcus had been seeing her and Max had been irresistibly attracted to her. Alexis. He had been tempted many times to pursue her but had always found the strength to resist the urge because she was with Marcus. At the time, Max had told himself that he would look her up if and when they broke up, but Max had lost contact and forgotten all about her. Maybe she was the one that got away. Maybe she was the one that could've made Max settle down and stop skirt chasing. If only he had met her instead of Nanna, maybe everything would be different. There were a lot of "maybes."

He turned a page and there was a faded photo of him with Alexis and Marcus with some others on a camping trip. Max noted the extra hair on his forehead and lack of age lines. They all held bottles of beer in various stages of fullness. Back in those days they used to drink a lot. Probably more than a lot. He remembered that on this particular binge he had passed out in his sleeping bag under the stars. When he awoke the next morning, the birds in the trees were starved for attention, screaming their little heads off so others would notice them. Max's jaw ached from gaping open all night long and a space-age epoxy had sealed his eyes shut. Prying them open, he was startled to find Alexis sitting right next to him, staring at him. He was a little disturbed by the creepy attention, but he liked her a lot so he got over it quickly. As he struggled to find something to say, she started speaking.

"I know you pretend to be a guy that pretends to be nice, but you actually truly *are* nice. There. I've discovered your secret. Don't worry, I won't tell anyone."

Without another word, she gave him a slight half-smile and turned and walked away. No matter how hard he wracked his brain, he could not think of anything kind he had done that would compel her to say something like that. He was never able to figure it out, and it was one of those compliments that stayed with him his whole life, never forgotten.

Memories were a marvel to Max. He often thought about how oddly human memory worked. We only remember the good or the bad, never the mediocre, mundane, or boring. We'll remember some flattering comment a cashier said to us in a grocery store twenty years ago, or we'll remember Marcy Turlington humiliating us in the cafeteria in the eighth grade, but we won't remember pushing an elevator button in a department store last week, or ten years ago making a mental note to clean the kitchen because you noticed a spot of Ragu on the counter. What we remember is pain, happiness, hurt feelings, and having fun. We do not remember clipping our toe nails, accidentally selecting the wrong grade when filling our car with gas, taking the kinks out of the phone cord, or scratching an itch on our leg during a seminar. If we add up all of those moments we can really remember, well, Max pondered, all of which are fleeting seconds, how much of our life will we actually recall when we're at the end of it? We'll have lived eighty years but only remember eleven months of it in total? As he closed the photo album on Alexis's beautiful face, he wondered if he'd remember that action five years from now.

A key entered the front door lock, the knob turned, and Max forgot all about Marcus's ex-girlfriend and the camping trip.

"You're home early."

Marcus came in; light and dust motes streaming in around him like a dirty halo.

"I thought you might be here. I left you the note, and decided to come home early. What's going on?"

Max brought him up to date. It took a while. Max started with the nude present he had found in his bed. Marcus was extremely envious. Apparently he had had a crush on the famous author's granddaughter for fifteen years. After Marcus finally calmed down, Max was able to continue his story. He was hesitant about including the part where he may or may not have poisoned Jimmy T., but as he was recounting his adventure, he decided on sharing it. While Max had been talking, the local news had come on, but the two had not paid attention. As Max's story reached its conclusion they became aware of the news program when they heard Jimmy T.'s name mentioned.

"…the famed Texas oil millionaire, known for his flamboyant and gruff manner in business, was found dead in San Diego's downtown train terminal." The anchorwoman's head partially blocked a green-screen image of Jimmy T. Glick's face playing peek-a-boo over her shoulder.

Murder was now added to the list of Max's sins. He couldn't believe it. A hollow, empty feeling started to form in the pit of his stomach and spread throughout his body. If he counted Ronzo and Silvia, his body count was up to three.

Marcus looked at him, glassy-eyed, with his mouth open, gaping.

The anchorwoman continued, "A knife was the likely weapon. The police are withholding any further comment until the coroner's report is final."

The hollow feeling in Max's stomach was replaced by extreme confusion. It was as if something he knew his whole life to be true, like the world being round, was suddenly revealed to be a lie, and he had to readjust his belief to accommodate a square earth.

"My God," Max stammered. "How? When? I don't understand."

"This is insane, Max. You have got to get out of the country. It's amazing that you've stayed alive this long. These people are assassins! They have no scruples at all!"

"I know, I know," Max agreed, "but I really need to make some sense of all this."

"Max! Think. Your choices are simple: you stay, you die. You leave, you have a chance. I will go with you if that's what it will take to get you the hell out of here."

Max wasn't listening. He was reflecting on the last few hours.

"It has to be Susan," he mumbled to himself. "Moris is in Spain. Susan is the only suspect left. She followed us when we left the apartment. He was a sitting duck there on the bench, all drugged up. Susan probably thought he was asleep and just sat on the bench next to him and casually stuck a knife in him. No one would've even noticed."

Marcus walked into the kitchen and said over his shoulder, "I'm packing. You can wear my clothes if you need something, but we're getting out of here tonight. Thanks for doing the dishes."

Max stared off into space.

"We'll be on the road in an hour, Max."

"Let's wait till tomorrow."

"What?"

"I need time to think."

The television camera switched from the female news anchor to the male. His gravelly bass betrayed that he cared little for the news item he read, as he had reported many similar stories over the course of his broadcasting career.

"An Imperial Beach man and a Chula Vista woman were found dead today in a scrap-metal recycling plant located in the three hundred block of Industrial Court in National City. Police think that they may have died yesterday while in a domestic fight involving a gun while arguing next to a defective railing. The act was caught on surveillance video."

"Oh good God," Max said to himself, feeling his stomach drop out from under him.

Grainy static blipped on and off like the camera was struggling to work. The screen filled with the image of Ronzo's backside from the shoulders down. The double crack of his gun being fired, and then he flew backward into the camera, his back growing larger and larger until he collided. Once again the snowy static came on and off, flickering madly, and then died out. The image began to play again, this time in slow motion. Max squinted hard at the set, and he could make out Silvia's body over Ronzo's shoulder. She staggered backward, chubby arms flailing about, until she bowled over Ronzo and the two took the camera out of commission. Max was nowhere to be seen in the video, completely blocked by the two bodies hurling toward the camera.

The recording began to roll again, this time with voice-over. "The surveillance camera, mounted on the railing at the top of the staircase, unfortunately had been neglected for many years and only sporadically worked, due to a short in its wiring. The pressure of the struggle on the floor boards jostled the railing, which moved the wiring enough for police to capture this few scant seconds of video. It's unclear why the woman had her back to her boyfriend, who held a gun, but it can be seen that she clearly threw herself at him in the struggle. The woman died from gunshot wounds and the young man died from a broken neck. One cryptic note in this is that the woman was a recently fired employee of millionaire Jimmy T. Glick. Police have found no connection as yet to link the deaths with the murder of her former employer. The victims' names will be released tomorrow."

"What do you make of that?" Marcus asked.

Max sighed heavily. "It seems I have another story to tell you."

18

A little past midnight, Max heard a sound at the front door. He was lying in the dark, sprawled across the couch, with the TV on for light, while he studied the ceiling and wondered how long dumb luck usually lasted. The sound didn't startle him, but it definitely did concern him. Headlights of a passing car briefly silhouetted a female form in the front window. The doorknob jiggled a little, and then a rap came at the door. *Suddenly there came a tapping, as of someone gently rapping, rapping at my chamber door.*

Max quietly got off the couch and went to the window. The woman outside had on faded jeans and a windbreaker. Her back was to him, but Max could recognize Moris's figure anywhere. So there were two suspects for

Jimmy's murder after all. Life was never simple.

He opened the door.

"I thought you were in Spain."

"Yeah, that's what Susan wanted. I woke up one morning drugged and with no ID or belongings. I had a hell of a time getting out of that country."

"How in the world did you find me?" Max queried.

"I hired a private detective to trail you."

"Or you're friends with Ronzo and Silvia. Or you trailed me yourself from the train station."

"Silvia...? What train station?"

"The one downtown. The one where you left Jimmy T.'s corpse rotting."

"Jimmy T. is dead?"

Max didn't feel that her question deserved a response. He was sick of all the games. The last time he had this same conversation with her in Spain he had lost his temper. All he had felt then was rage, but this time he felt exhausted and ill, like he had some kind of a flu. A dull pain began to throb behind his right eye.

Turning his back on Moris, Max moved to the couch. When he had seated himself and looked up again, she was holding a small pistol. It looked like a toy in her hand and instilled absolutely no fear in him. It could have easily been made of plastic. He couldn't really tell from where he sat.

"Sorry, Max, but I need the suitcase. Susan must have killed Jimmy, and that's fine with me because it's one less person I need to worry about."

Without consciously thinking about his movements, Max got off the sofa, covered the distance to Moris in two steps, and effortlessly took the handgun away from her.

"I'm sick of you, I'm sick of Susan, I'm glad Jimmy is dead, but most of all I want you out of my life." Max felt his temper rising to an uncontrollable state and his feeling of exhaustion was left far behind. This, he thought, had better be the last time he was on the receiving end of a pistol. "Come on."

"Where are we going?"

"I'm giving you the manuscript. After that I don't want to see any of you people again."

He grabbed Moris by the arm and with his gun hand pushed her out the door. All the way down the path to his car he lectured her about people pulling guns on him, lying to him, and generally making him crazy. The chance to lecture made him feel good.

As he reached the curb, Max felt something jump out from its hiding place behind him along the hedge that bordered the sidewalk. As he turned he felt a lightning bolt jolt through his head, and as he blacked out he heard glass tinkling around him.

......

When Max awoke, he had a horrible headache and a tremendous kink in his neck. Trying to get his eyeballs to cooperate and focus, he realized that he was in the back seat of a car. A woman with dark shoulder-length hair was driving. Most likely Moris. Max panned his eyes sideways to the passenger seat and saw a small feminine hand holding a revolver on the driver. More guns, he thought.

Great. Forcing his eyes to travel painfully up the arm, he found his way to Susan's lovely face, which didn't look particularly lovely at that moment. She wore a very menacing expression.

"What's the story, morning glory?" Susan said, realizing that Max was conscious.

"Ggnk," Max offered in response.

"Geez, I didn't realize I hit you so hard."

"You didn't have to clobber me, you know? I was taking Moris to the suitcase of my own free will."

"Didn't know that, sport. I'm assuming it's at the train station, so we're headed in that direction."

"So it *was* you that killed Jimmy."

"No comment, kiddo," Susan said with a big smile that confessed much pride. "I *will* let you know, however, who killed that publisher in Bath," she added with a dramatic glance at Moris.

"Shut up, Susan," Moris spoke for the first time since Max had been awake. "You're a born liar. Don't drag me into your-"

"That means you did the one in Spain, as well," Max threw out to Susan.

"Again, no comment."

"Life is cheap to you," Max said with a disgusted sneer.

"I will do whatever it takes to get that book back in the family. We need it. It's our legacy."

Clinical depression and craziness is your legacy, Max thought to himself.

......

They parked outside, along the curb, near the entrance of the station. The streetlights looked muted behind the fog that had glided in from the harbor. There wasn't much traffic on the street, and even less foot traffic on the sidewalks. A few homeless people were sleeping under blankets up and down the street.

"All right," Susan began, "we all three go in together. Remember, I have a gun."

"So no funny business, see?" Max joked bitterly, sounding like a combination of Cagney and Bogart and Edward G. Robinson.

As they climbed out of the car, Max noticed that Susan was wearing a mid-length pea coat, like a sailor. Her hand was in her left pocket, and it bulged a little more than it should. They walked through the double doors, Susan falling back a bit behind them.

Max glanced around the lobby. The service windows were all closed up with Next Window Please signs stuck in them. A security guard was sleeping in one of the hard plastic chairs attached to the far wall. Max stopped and looked at the two women. Moris stared blankly back at him, and Susan raised her eyebrows as if to say, "Get on with it."

It had been a fun ride, Max thought, even though he had complained the whole time. Both women were beautiful and exciting. He went to exotic locales and had an adventure, complete with murder and intrigue. What more could a man want? Now it was coming to an end, and there was the distinct possibility that he could end up dead, but for some reason he wasn't a nervous wreck about it anymore. Maybe he had been beaten down and was just too tired and jaded to give a damn. Or maybe he was just getting good at the game, every bit as professional as Moris and Susan, maybe even better.

Pulling the key out of his pocket, Max approached the locker for the second time in twenty-four hours. The door swung outward and Max peered into the gloom of the baggage compartment. Most of the small suitcase was shrouded by shadow, but the overhead lights of the station lit the bottom corner of it. So much fuss, he thought, about an old dilapidated bag. Grabbing the handle, he pulled it out and swung around. Moris and Susan were standing close together next to a nearby bench.

"Here it is," Max said, a little louder than he usually spoke. "I hope it was worth it. I hope it was worth killing for."

"Get outside, *now*," Susan hissed between clenched teeth.

Max shrugged his shoulders and walked on past the two, dragging his feet. They left the lonely station in single file, with Susan bringing up the rear. When they reached the car, Susan decided to change the seating assignments from their previous road trip: Max was to drive, Moris was in the back, and Susan had shotgun…literally.

"Where to?"

"Head over to Market Street," Susan said, the gun now out of its pocket and aimed at his ribs.

Max moved the steering wheel easily from side to side, relaxed as if he were on a Sunday drive. How shallow I am, he thought. I've been writing my own novel, which is shallow as can be, and I have lived an adventure, which is like a shallow man's dream, and now that I'm probably approaching death, it's only fitting that I die an empty needless death. No one will know about it, no one will notice me gone. No one will mourn my passing. My toe tag will read: John Doe #414.

"Make a right here," Susan said, motioning at a seedy liquor store that covered a large lot on the street corner.

Max made the turn and noted that there were very few streetlights and that most of them were burnt out. They drove past many homeless people asleep on the street, and a few abandoned vehicles. The fog shrouded most of the scenery, but Max could tell they were moving into an unsavory neighborhood. Loading docks sandwiched them in on both sides, and soon they stopped seeing sleeping bodies and Max understood why. They were in a secluded warehouse district.

"Pull over, right here."

Max followed her orders and parked next to a raised dock with the remnants of smashed vegetables smeared across it. As he put the gear lever in park, his seat bucked violently forward, Susan's gun flew across the dash, and he and she got pitched into the windshield. Righting himself, Max saw that Moris had lunged across Susan's headrest and wrapped her arms around Susan's neck in a chokehold. Susan stopped trying to free herself from Moris's grip when she saw Max's attention drawn to the gun on the dash and flung her arms out to intercept it. Her reach was too short and Max snatched it up quickly.

Even though Max had the gun leveled at Susan, he knew that he had no intention of using it. It wasn't in him. The death of Silvia and Ronzo was accidental. It wasn't his intention that they go over the railing. Even when he thought he was poisoning Jimmy T., it was only a matter of survival, or self-defense. And at that, too, he had been holding out hope that he was just putting Jimmy to sleep.

The thing that amazed Max was that even though he saw Susan's movements in slow motion, it was still too fast for him to do anything. The scene in the cramped car instantly turned into a bad Sam Peckinpah movie, alternating between slow motion and quick snippets of ultra-fast movement. Susan reached into her pea coat and pulled out a revolver— which Max later recognized as Moris's gun, which Susan must have taken off him when she knocked him out cold behind the hedge. She brought it up in a smooth motion, snapped the barrel of it over her shoulder, and fired it directly into Moris's face.

The shock, the horror, the fear of it all made him fire too. The passenger window exploded next to Susan's face. She screamed and reflexively dropped the gun. Max heard it bounce along the floor of the car and he knew he wouldn't need to worry about her retrieving it. Broken glass spilled out as Susan threw the door open and climbed out with the suitcase. The last Max ever saw of her, except for a picture in *Time* magazine much later, was her black pea coat fading off into the San Diego fog.

Moris lay dead in the back seat, rolled on her side. He didn't turn her over. He didn't want to see the damage that had been done to her face. Two shots had been fired. Someone had to hear them. The liquor store wasn't that far away, and the homeless people were even closer. It probably wouldn't be too long before the police showed up.

He wasn't certain what had his fingerprints on it and what didn't. Max didn't want to try and wipe down the car and then later worry about whether or not he got it all. The police needed very little these days to track someone down, and he didn't want

Susan twisting things around and implicating him in any of the murders. Going up against her and trying to get her to pay for her crimes would only backfire on him. Deep down he suspected that she was probably much cleverer than him, and in the end he would be the one in the electric chair. He had to trust that another form of punishment would bite her in the ass.

The car was still running. Max pushed in the cigarette lighter, and while it was heating up, he tore off the tail end of his shirt. When the lighter popped out red hot he climbed out of the car and walked around to the gas tank. Stuffing the rag into the tank he ignited the end of it.

As Max walked off into the warehouse district, he looked over his shoulder and saw the side of the car go up in flames. A few moments later the fire spread internally through the car and exploded.

The damp air sent a chill through Max. He thought of Moris's beautiful, destroyed face as he trudged through the streets and alleys. She was bad most of the way through, cold, conniving, dishonest. And even though she wasn't a friend, there was still something he very much had liked about her. He enjoyed the intimate stories she shared with him, that one intimate moment in Spain at the table on the street. The stories very well may have been invented, or belonged to someone else, but he preferred to believe it was really her opening up and feeling comfortable with him. He enjoyed her occasional attempts at sarcasm. And she was so beautiful. What a waste of a human life. It was a waste how she lived it and a waste how she went out. But who was he to judge?

19

Basically, the *Time* magazine article stated that the beautiful granddaughter of America's most celebrated author was going to prison for forgery. She had passed off a story of a man who falls in love with an immigrant while working at a condom factory as a long-lost manuscript written by her grandfather. The critics were amazed. They couldn't believe how the publishers of the book had actually thought that the novel was authentic. The Old Man would never have written something so shallow. True enough, it was heavily influenced by him, but it was definitely not scribed by his hand.

In the courtroom it came out that Susan couldn't account for how she came across her grandfather's manuscript. When she produced the alleged document, it was proven to be typed on modern laser copy paper and printed from a computer printer. The handwritten notes in the margins didn't come close to matching the Old Man's handwriting at all.

Max smiled. Susan would be going to jail after all. Of course, he laid it all out in his head that it would happen that way when he had substituted his tawdry story for the real McCoy, but to see it actually work out the way he had planned brought him genuine pleasure.

Max tucked the rolled magazine under his arm and strolled out of the newsstand and down the street. He couldn't believe that a year had passed since he was mixed up with the two women and the crazy Texan. It was all so clear in his mind. He could clearly see himself leaving the burning car in the fog. He could see himself going back to Marcus's little house by the beach. He could see himself counting off paces in the sand like a pirate with his map, and he could see himself on all fours digging in the sand, digging down to the plastic garbage bag containing the ream of yellowed paper.

Max had said his goodbyes to Marcus and a couple other friends that he would miss, and packed up and moved to New York. When he was in college he had always dreamed of moving to New York and becoming a writer, he had just never done it. Once in the city, he found himself a job, as copyeditor on a small struggling magazine that was trying to compete with *The New Yorker*, and set out to rebuild his life. A life with goals, and meaning. A couple of Max's short stories had found their way into print, and now he was trying his hand at a new novel. It was kind of nice that no one knew that his first published novel was a flop. But that novel was written by a different person, at least that's how Max looked at it. He had grown so much in the last twelve months.

Part of his growth involved a woman, a woman actually close to his own age, whom he was starting to build a serious relationship with. Life was uncomplicated and good. The only remnant of his complicated life was the manuscript.

When he had walked through the fog-enshrouded streets of San Diego after his first and hopefully last gun battle, he had decided that he wouldn't publish it. The world didn't know what it was missing, and Max would cherish the book as his own private treasure. Thomas Willburry-Sleeveridge, the previous owner, must have been doing just that with the manuscript before he passed away. Max wondered if he, too, had had to go through hell and two treacherous women to get it.

The End

www.ingramcontent.com/pod-product-compliance
Lightning Source LLC
Chambersburg PA
CBHW062025170626
46813CB00001B/294